To Lisa
with love
& duckness
(but not
too much :)
— Tim
19/8/1998

GW00339476

DUCKNESS

Tim Richards is the author of
Letters to Francesca (1996) and
The Prince (1997)

Duckness

Tim Richards

ALLEN & UNWIN

This project has been assisted by the Commonwealth Government through the Australia Council, its arts funding and advisory body.

First published in 1998 by
Allen & Unwin
9 Atchison Street, St Leonards NSW 2065 Australia
Phone: (61 2) 8425 0100
Fax: (61 2) 9906 2218
E-mail: frontdesk@allen-unwin.com.au
Web: http://www.allen-unwin.com.au

National Library of Australia
Cataloguing-in-Publication entry:

Richards, Tim, 1960– .
  Duckness.

  ISBN 1 86448 761 5.

  I. Title

A823.3

Set in 10/13 pt Palatino by DOCUPRO, Sydney
Printed and bound by Australian Print Group, Maryborough, Victoria

10 9 8 7 6 5 4 3 2 1

CONTENTS

The great question of the twentieth (century) is the co-existence of different concepts of time.

Sunless, Chris Marker

The quantum world is almost timeless. Things don't seem to happen in sequence. Everything is about relationship, ebbing and flowing together. It becomes unreal to talk about before and after: you can't say that this happened before that happened.

'Quantum Physics and Motherhood', Danah Zohar

DUCKNESS

And he seemed to become more
Australian and apathetic each week.
The great indifference, the darkness of
the fern-world, upon his mind. Then
spurts of energy, spurts of sudden
violent desire, spurts of gambling
excitement. But the mind in a kind of
twilight sleep.

D.H. Lawrence, *Kangaroo*

Rebecca in The House of Eggs

When she wasn't reading, or thinking about the novel she
ought to be writing, Rebecca sat in the lounge and contemplated the dust. She was thinking about the dust when her
father called out from his bedroom.

Are my eggs ready? he yelled.

No, I haven't cooked them yet. I was hoping you might
have died.

Rebecca timed his pause: one, two, three, four . . .

Not fried, *poached*, her father yelled.

3

This place is held together by the dust, she thought. And it's all that's holding him together. If I dusted him, no one could ever prove it was murder.

Rebecca considered these possibilities, but she knew she'd lost the will to intervene. The thought of dusting overwhelmed her.

The only place in the house not ruled by the dust was the kitchen. The kitchen was ruled by grease. Rebecca picked up the frying pan, tilting it to spread a barely fluid layer of fat. She lit the gas beneath the pan, broke two eggs on the rim, and watched the contents dive into the crackling fat.

I'm frying you some eggs, she yelled.

Poached! I wanted poached! came the reply.

I'll poach some in my spit, if you like. One, two, three . . .

Just make sure you don't break the yolks.

Rebecca watched the egg whites crisp at the edges. A cloud of greasy vapour rose out of the pan. She opened the window above the sink, just as a silver train rumbled past on its way to Hampton station. When the train left her view, Rebecca could see across to the red-brick wall on the other side of the tracks. Many years ago, vandals with white paint had daubed **NO FUTURE** on the wall.

Those old-style punks with their English influences had long since given way to American-style graffiti gangs. The brats in baseball caps will be down soon to paint over the top of that, Rebecca thought. They'll paint it over with the swirly New York-style graffiti that only the artists and their mates can read. The new gangs couldn't give a shit that there's no future. The pseudo-American brats will spray the punks and their anarchy into nonexistence.

Rebecca picked up the egg flipper, drove the metal tip of it into the egg yolks, and watched the yellow dribble across the bubbling white.

I'm sorry, Dad, the yolks broke, Rebecca yelled.

Waiting on Godot

Dad's terminal, her brother Trevor had said.

At the time, Rebecca understood this to mean that her father was terminally ill, that her father was on the verge of death. She took three months' leave from teaching, believing that someone ought to be there to see him out.

Yes, Dad's Terminal, Rebecca thought, as she pulled a dusty paperback from one of the bookshelves in the lounge. What Trevor really meant, she now realised, was that I should live here in Dad's Terminal, that I should dedicate my life to his dust.

Rebecca remembered standing before her Year 12 English class to explain that she was taking three months' compassionate leave. She would be back, she promised, well before their exams.

But Miss Parker, George Soutanis complained, your father's gotta die sooner or later. If we fail English, the rest of our lives are up shit creek.

Denise Sutton, who hardly ever said anything, said, It's probably not even true that your father's dying. You're probably taking a trip to the Greek islands.

If only she had escaped to the Greek islands.

When three months passed, Rebecca chose to resign, and promised herself that she would write a book while caring for her father. She intended to write a grand tale of risk and adventure, a novel which rehearsed in fine detail the kind of life that she would lead when her father died.

But her father didn't die, and Rebecca seldom attempted to address an empty page. She was often forced to consider the possibility that she had taken on the nursing role as a deliberate distraction. With an invalid father to care for, she had an excuse not to challenge her fear of sexual involvements, or her fear of failing to achieve a great literary ambition.

Four years passed. Four years attending to a man who ate little other than eggs, toast, chipped potatoes and sausages. He never once thanked her for her efforts, and she learnt to measure time in the frying, scrambling, and poaching of his eggs.

Give these pillows a bashing, will you? There's a lumpity bit boggling the muscles in my back.

Speak English to me! she'd explode. This pig-Irish drivel gives me the shits!

But Rebecca's anger was wasted on the apparently healthy man in the blue-and-white pinstriped pyjamas. She thumped his pillows, propped him up against them, and tried not to notice the perspiration rings expanding under his arms. And always when she was at the peak of some unspoken exasperation, he would ask about her work-in-progress.

How goes the novel?

The novel! How do you imagine that I could write in this place? It's impossible to work here.

No, you're right, he'd say, Australia is impossible now. Australians blame everything that's gone wrong on the Japs or the Yanks, but we still crawl to them, and beg them to set things right. It's impossible to work here.

Finally, Rebecca turned her attention to the paperback she had selected. She slapped the book against her thigh to shift the dust. The novel was *Women in Love* by D.H. Lawrence. Inside the front cover was the biro inscription,

Rebecca Parker
Year 12
Hampton High
Tel. 98–5977

The Virgin and The Duck Hunter

Rebecca was seventeen, and in her final year at high school, when she first read *Women in Love*. She considered that she had been opened up by D.H. Lawrence. After reading Lawrence, she had looked at the football heroes who were lusted after by the other girls in the class, and she was unable to imagine how they could excite love, the real passionate love she yearned for.

Lawrence breathed emotion. He wasn't frightened of excesses, or contradictions, or confusions, or repetitions. Lawrence wasn't distant like the other authors she had read. He wrote like someone who had got his hands dirty.

Rebecca had consumed *Women in Love* in one long sitting, and read *The Rainbow* the next weekend. For class that Monday, she had prepared seven foolscap pages of notes.

Rebecca's teacher, Mr Longreach, was an informal, charismatic type. The girls in his class liked to speculate about whether Mr Longreach wore underpants beneath his tight, faded-blue jeans. The consensus was that Mr Longreach did not wear underpants. Instead of sitting on a chair behind his desk, Mr Longreach liked to sit on the desk, with one foot drawn up onto the table surface, so that he leaned slightly to one side.

Rebecca could still picture Mr Longreach as he appeared that Monday, his copy of *Women in Love* held up to the class. He asked who hadn't finished reading the novel, and the usual stragglers put up their hands. Mr Longreach sent them to the library.

Someone had asked, maybe it was Frank Sheehan, why the class had to study *Women in Love*. Whoever it was told Mr Longreach that *Women in Love* was a bucket of shit.

Rebecca had waited for the teacher's reply.

She thought that she had seen Mr Longreach's crotch bulge slightly at that moment. He took on a very serious expression. Yes, I'm sad to say that *Women in Love* by D.H. Lawrence is a piece of wet, highly overrated crap.

Rebecca, in her distress, had seen the football boys enjoy this immensely.

Can anyone tell me what the D.H. in D.H. Lawrence stands for? Mr Longreach asked.

Rebecca might have suggested Dark Hedonist, but Simon Burton got in first with Dick Head. Mr Longreach called this a good try, but pointed out that dickhead was one word not two. He had gone on to say that he had the misfortune to study D.H. Lawrence at university. He and his colleagues used to refer to Lawrence as the Duck Hunter, owing to an idiosyncrasy of his prose.

Even pretentious old droners like T.S. Eliot never droned on like Lawrence, Mr Longreach told the class. Lawrence isn't a writer. Lawrence is a jackhammer. Mr Longreach chose as his example the way that Lawrence used the words 'dark' and 'darkness'.

Rebecca remembered she had asked whether that wasn't to do with sexual apprehensiveness, but her teacher replied that it would have been all right to use the words in that fashion once or twice; Lawrence didn't know when to stop.

Mr Longreach had asked the class if they knew how many times Lawrence used the words 'dark', 'darkening' and 'darkness' in *Women in Love*.

Two-hundred-and-fifteen times! he said. I've counted them! The world drowned in darkness, the magnetic darkness, the potent darkness, the innermost dark marrow of the body, the voluptuous resonance of darkness, the waves of darkness, the suave loins of darkness.

Mr Longreach told the class that Lawrence was a fraud, ridiculous and irrational, and Rebecca was furious she hadn't been able to counter then as she would now, that passion *is* irrational, fierce, and ridiculous.

Mr Longreach went on to tell the class that he and his mates had parodied Lawrence's extravagance by substituting the word 'duck' wherever 'dark' appeared. They called themselves the Duck Hunters, the assassins of pretentiousness.

Everything begins to slide off into the duckness, Mr

Longreach went on, delighting in his own legendary status, into the great stormy duckness above the great duck void. You are met with a profound duckness, a fire of the chill night breaking constantly onto the pure duckness, the unknown duckness.

Rebecca had watched her teacher recite all two-hundred-and-fifteen known instances of duck and duckness, and she had felt consumed with simultaneous fury and embarrassment. She begged the bell to ring, feeling slightly ashamed that her emotional virginity had been given up to a man being lampooned as a duck hunter.

She remembered Longreach's dumb-arrogant comments at the bottom of the essay that she wrote on *Women in Love*— *Naive, impressionable girls are always sucked in by Lawrence. You must learn to combat this sort of pomposity by taking the mickey, Rebecca. You need to explore your inner duckness.*

Now, when Rebecca returned to the opening lines of *Women in Love*, she did so determined to reclaim the darkness for Lawrence; David Herbert Lawrence, the man who knew more about passion and conviction than any man or duck hunter she had ever known in Melbourne.

A Duckness Embraces Professor Sharp

Rebecca remembered the day that her brother Trevor was appointed Professor of Australian Literature at the University. After rushing out to buy a set of polo-necked jumpers and matching jackets, he saw a hair consultant, and he exchanged his black-rimmed glasses for contact lenses. Trevor even asked Rebecca whether he should trade in his ancient motorcycle for something more in keeping with his new office.

Trevor liked to zoom through the southern suburbs of Melbourne on his Triumph, wearing a long red scarf that trailed in the wind. Rebecca advised him to keep the bike, that it would help him to retain the common touch, but what she really hoped was that Trevor would be intercepted by the police, and booked for not wearing a helmet. Rebecca wanted to see her brother brought down a notch or two.

Trevor was a clever man, devious enough to overcome his lack of imagination or insight by reading the inclination of the wind. He had the knack of discovering some crucial piece of dirt that he could hold over an empowering agent.

Once a fortnight, Trevor roared up the driveway. He always claimed that he was visiting his father, and he would leave a stack of books to be read, but it was rare for Trevor to enter his father's room.

Trevor would place his books on the table in the lounge, telling Rebecca, You ought to dust this place. When did this place last have a good dusting?

You'll be buried by this dust, Trevor once told her. What you really need is to get out of this crypt now and then. You need a bit of invigoration. A good shagging wouldn't do you any harm.

Rebecca had wanted to say, You condemned me to this, so don't come goose-stepping in here to tell me what I need, though the idea of a good shagging did appeal to her. What she had actually said was, It's *my* life. She knew that if she hit Trevor, he would have that to use against her when the moment suited him.

Rebecca, could you scramble me some eggs? a voice called from down the corridor.

She will in just a few minutes, Dad, Trevor replied.

Rebecca turned her back on Trevor, but he refused to notice.

If you tidied this place up, you'd see things differently. You might even get to work on that novel of yours.

When Rebecca turned, Trevor was flicking through her copy of *Women in Love*.

It's reading this crap that makes you so overwrought, Trevor observed.

Rebecca was used to Trevor ridiculing her taste in fiction. So, what masterworks of Australian literature are you teaching these days? she asked.

Masterworks went out with Leavis, Trevor said. We take seminars in sporting autobiography, narrative structure in television soap opera, advertising strategies in women's magazines, and the role of the duck in Michael Leunig's cartoons. We've got a fabulous seminar that compares notions of optimism and free will in Australian horoscopes with their American counterparts. None of these kids want to read novels, least of all Australian novels. We're well past the time when you can have an elite hierarchising the importance and worth of things according to elite values. We analyse the forms and genres that the public chooses to consume. We take ordinary values seriously.

Rebecca felt like she had missed something. This was Trevor, the same Trevor who had spent seven years writing an unpublished thesis on sexual metaphor in Shakespeare, now claiming to champion the interests of the common Australian.

But where are the leaders going to come from? she asked. Who is going to create values, and question values, if you've got the brightest students in the country convinced that the only thing worth doing is reading French theorists in translation and gazing up their own arse? We need universities to be creating an audience for original thought, for writers and critics who can offer alternative versions of Australian society, and future societies, not just using Gallic hocus-pocus to rationalise the way things are.

You've got us wrong, Trevor said. We have a different sort of doctor teaching in the English Department. We don't prescribe. We don't exclude or belittle.

No, and you never take any responsibility either.

Trevor stayed for a cup of tea, as he usually did. He suggested that Rebecca could go back to teaching, and still care for their father, so long as she organised her time properly. He told her that she would have written her book already if she was ever going to be a writer.

Rebecca watched from the window as Trevor kick-started his Triumph, revving it long enough to annoy her neighbours. Finally, he moved off, and Rebecca waited to see the very last of the beam of light which cut a path through Trevor's duckness.

Trevor's bike could still be heard in the distance, shifting gear in South Road, when Rebecca called out to her father, Do you want me to scramble some eggs?

An omelette.

An omelette then, Rebecca yelled.

Yes, an omelette.

Opening the window to the cool night air, Rebecca heard young voices from the other side of the railway line. The gang of brats with their spray cans had arrived. Rebecca was so pleased with the accuracy of her prediction that for a moment she didn't hear the other voice, the voice filling her head with words and phrases that were forming themselves into complete sentences. At first, she tried to organise the words in her head, but soon she realised that there would be too many to recall. She put aside her mixing bowl and reached for a pen.

An hour passed.

Ignoring the bellows from her father, Rebecca sat to read the paragraphs that she had written. She knew it wasn't masterly prose, but it was the beginning of a story that she would have to complete.

It was Professor Sharp's fashion to address the shiest female students in his tutorial when asking questions which related to the use of vulgarisms or sexual euphemism in a literary text.

What do you make of the word 'wick' in this context? he asked the crimson-cheeked Anna.

Stella, perhaps you could tell the class what this word 'coynte' refers to?

When Stella dissolved into tears, the Professor spoke without sympathy, I don't think that's necessary. We're adults here.

Professor Sharp was a strangely contradictory man. Though he delighted in telling embarrassed young women that coynte referred to cunt, and that a fetching woman was one who made a man come, he was steadfast in his contempt for modern female writers who punctuated their fiction with immodest description or the language of the streets.

For several years, he kept displayed in his classroom a photocopy of a review in which he assailed a young novelist for showing no more skill than the harlot's capacity to talk dirty, and he made clear his opinion that her preoccupation with unconventional sex was an outrage to public decency. Her novel was unfit to be classed as literature.

The subsequent fame of this writer did nothing to undermine the Professor's confidence in his judgment. In fact, nothing unnerved Professor Sharp until he came into contact with a second-year student named Catherine O'Shaunessy.

Catherine was an outwardly shy, round-shouldered blonde. She had exactly the kind of prettiness that ordinarily attracted the Professor's interest. During the first tutorial of the year, Professor Sharp liked to sound out his new students with a passage of poetry, and he chose to ask Catherine what the word 'quaint' meant.

Catherine ran her finger beneath the line on the photocopied handout. She looked at the phrase for a moment, before removing her glasses to look Professor Sharp in the eye.

You might not realise this, Catherine told the Professor, but the combination of your bald head, and that polo-necked jumper, makes you look exactly like a penis with ears.

As her father continued to wail about his omelette, Rebecca scribbled a title above the opening to her story. The first thing that came to mind was 'Modern Education', but she quickly discarded that to replace it with a working title that always made her smile whenever she considered the work-in-progress, 'A Duckness Embraces Professor Sharp'

August 18th, 1998 -

Dear Lisa,

Finally scraped together the $ to buy one of these. Overpricing is one of its many problems. (I hope you can fund something worthwhile in it. Not much to report since I last wrote. While Essendons winning, all is well in the world.

Be happy, smile lots.

(LOVE)

Tim -

BOTERO
La Sieste - 1982 - *The Nap*
Editions Hazan, Paris © F. Botero
1731

DIDO

Now that I'm older, I can see that my life has been blessed with certain advantages. If you lined up all the people who had ever lived on this planet, 999 out of 1000 would choose to swap places with me. The dead ones especially. My problem is that I was never taught to appreciate the many wonderful objects and opportunities given to me, or to appreciate my generally advantaged situation in life.

It always comes down to love. My parents mistook gifts and expensive schools and clothes for genuine affection. I'm not saying it's their fault that I grew up to be the person I did, or that they failed to care about the kind of person I became. Despite their wealth, my parents are fine people. They must have wanted their only son to mature into a man with a true appreciation of life and his place in it. Even now, when I am supposedly adult, they still seek to remedy the situation. They feel guilty that they never gave me enough time. They know that time, in the final analysis, is all that parents can give their children. Through Miss Bartlett, my parents hope to give me the kind of time they never had time to give.

Governesses are rare in Melbourne. I would venture to suggest that I am the only thirty-seven-year-old man in this city who has his own governess. Which isn't to mock the situation. I am learning to become less cynical and more appreciative. It may well turn out that I am the forerunner of a new breed; wealthy, emotionally immature men who have their practical and moral concerns managed by a well-qualified intermediary.

Miss Cassandra Bartlett (she refuses to let me call her Cassie) is an extremely well-qualified young woman. Her mother is a Tetley, of tea fame, and her father has a seat in the House of Lords. The Bartlett family own a fine home in Woodstock, and are related to the Churchills by marriage. Having attended finishing school in Zurich, Miss Bartlett took a three-year course in domestic instruction at the prestigious Fothergill College in South London, returning the following year to write her Honours thesis, 'A Systematic Approach to Late-Adolescent Hygiene', since published as *The Enemy Between The Folds*. As the dux of her year, Miss Bartlett would have been destined for a well-remunerated position in one of the Arab states until my mother approached her with a challenge no ambitious governess could refuse.

Though she is a slender, softly spoken woman, with a complexion typical of the English upper classes, an easy smile, and the prettiest strawberry-blonde hair, only a fool would take Miss Bartlett lightly. She is studied enough in her craft to command a respect and attention which belies her twenty-three years. When Miss Bartlett demands that I tidy my papers under threat of no pudding, I hustle. When she tells me I shall no longer be permitted to see or speak to Miranda Murray, on account of Miranda's uncouth telephone manner, I accept that Miss Bartlett's judgment, though harsh, constitutes my own best interest. But you mustn't imagine that our relationship is all instruction, critique, and interdiction. We have fun together. My governess is well-schooled in the science of fun.

While my parents believe that they failed me by not giving enough of their time, Miss Bartlett gives me nothing but time. My days are now broken up into regular, bite-sized chunks:

drawing lessons, music lessons, music appreciation, riding, physical instruction, exercise, free-reading, literature, speech lessons, philosophy, and argument. I can't imagine what I used to do with my time before Miss Bartlett arrived to organise it.

We discuss John Stuart Mill and Spinoza as if the future of truly important things like the Australian Tourist Industry or professional golf depended on it. She slaps the back of my left hand if I get lazy with my chords. She tempts me with old-fashioned foods like crusty homemade pies, and Yorkshire puddings. Miss Bartlett's potato gems are a delicacy beyond compare.

If the sun's out, we sit under the big liquidambar and she reads aloud from her favourite novels: *The Mill on the Floss*, *The Mayor of Casterbridge*, or *Emma*. On occasion, she will invite me to take her from behind as she reads. She is a great one for combining pleasures, and for choosing just the right patter to stir my blood.

You might like to raise my skirt and take me roughly while I read from Chapter Four.

Naturally, I accept her gentle invitations, though neither of us pretend that this is what my parents had in mind when they took the delicious Miss Bartlett into their employ. I dare say they wanted her to keep me out of trouble, to dissuade their son from dabbling with the stock market or cocaine, or a combination of the two. And indeed, she has succeeded in tempering the advance of my vices. I no longer gamble at the casino, or drink to excess, or spend long evenings slouched alone in front of the television. In fact, the television is always off now, to serve as a dark mirrored screen in case I need to see her reflected, naked above me, swivelling and grinding, managing me to a nicety. My serve of sticky pudding, as she so fetchingly refers to it.

I mustn't convey the impression that I always buckle to my parents' wishes, or bark at Miss Bartlett's command. I will not cease to be my own man merely because a young governess administers my time and reports back to my parents. Sometimes, I find it necessary to make a statement to that effect.

As we sit side by side at the keyboard, I seize Miss Bartlett's wrist, and direct her hand to the intruder in my trousers. This is the game she likes to describe as 'putting a collar on the dolphin'.

Richard, I shouldn't need to remind you that there is a time for games, and there is a time for piano practice, and it benefits neither of us to confuse the two.

The dolphin's awfully unhappy without his collar, Cassie.

I'm Miss Bartlett to you. If you continue to address me by the diminutive of my Christian name, I shall have to report back to your mother. I'll tell her that you've spoken impertinently. I'll tell her that you've made impertinent requests for gratification.

In which case, I shall have to advise the Academic Council of Fothergill College that their most illustrious graduate accedes to the sexual demands of the children in her charge. What would that do for your career, Miss Bartlett?

She opens my fly and runs a gentle finger down the underside of the agitated mammal.

Richard, I believe that you are trying to extort sexual favours from me.

It's extortion only if you believe it's extortion, Miss Bartlett.

But mostly I do as Miss Bartlett wishes because I could wish for nothing more. I like her best when she kisses me hungrily on the lips and calls me the young master, or when she is angry and threatens corporal punishment.

Curiously enough, her anger reminds me of my maternal grandmother. It fell to Omar, an energetic woman in her early sixties, to care for me while my parents scoured the deserts of north-western Kenya in search of ancient bones. Though I loved Omar fiercely, I felt her love most urgently when I provoked her anger. I would choose exactly the right moment to throw a tantrum in the aisle of a supermarket. It might have been about something so trivial as her disinclination to buy me a White Knight or a Bertie Beetle. I would shriek and wail.

Richard, if you don't stop it this very minute, you'll get Dido when we get home!

How I adored Omar's threats of Dido. The very word Dido was a thing of intricate beauty; more poetic enticement than the suggestion of an awful punishment to recoil from.

This Dido so often proved to be a wooden cooking implement whacked hard at the back of my fat thighs, a physically ambivalent experience that somehow combined rare excruciation and exhilaration. (At times when passions were less intense, I'd be allowed to lick cake mix off this same wooden spoon.)

I remember my beloved Omar red-faced, stretched beyond reason to this senseless violence, the spoon in motion, a fusion of sound, motion, and emotion that was Dido incarnate.

Dido might have meant something different to Omar than it meant to me. Dido was the thing I would get for being less than I could be. I'm telling you Richard, stop it this minute or you'll get Dido!

Dido was a credit voucher in the shop of things to come.

Maybe Miss Bartlett is the Dido that I'd always been promised. Her destiny is to take me to the other side of Dido, the dark place where punishment and reward are indistinguishable.

Yet I fear that Miss Bartlett won't stay. She's too professional to say so, but I know she hates the dusty north winds, and yearns for winter snow. She sits in front of the broad dresser in her bedroom and vigorously applies moisturisers and lotions. She rubs them into the back of her hands, and deep into her perfect cheeks. Sometimes, she lets me smother my own lips in rum 'n' raisin lip balm, and we kiss till her

21

lips say enough. But one day her lips will say enough is enough, and Miss Bartlett will head back to a leafy green corner of the Cotswolds.

On Sunday evening, she sits at the big table and writes her weekly report. My Shostakovich is coming along, I need to apply myself more to ball skills, I am generally tidy, mostly well-mannered, but still given to moments of selfish impetuosity. I must try to be more considerate with my pony, Wayne. My speech is showing the benefit of improved breathing and relaxation, and I am developing a more sophisticated understanding of God's role in the production and dissemination of evil. I have a good voice, but I must apply myself to my singing. I need to become more broadminded in my appreciation of literature.

I contest the latter point. This is the pot calling the kettle black. If only Miss Bartlett would allow me to read the moderns, or even the so-called postmoderns. I used to read Toni Morrison and David Ireland and James Ellroy before she arrived to regulate my reading. I argue that she should broaden her own outlook beyond Tolstoy, Turgenev, and Henry James.

But this unaccountable narrowness in her literary tastes contrasts with her adventurousness in the sensual arts. Most notably, she delights in a strange, rowboat-like position which bends my intent almost to snapping point, an exquisite, ineffable verge that might be Dido itself.

Oh baby, she coos. My baby. My baby.

This Dido is nothing compared to the Dido I will face when Miss Bartlett reports to her employers that I have acted immaturely and disgracefully. She will be forced to tell my parents that I have been pricking holes in condoms in the hope of securing her permanent governance of my time. Cassie, my darling, hear this confession. I'm a selfish scoundrel. I will deserve everything that I get.

STEVE WAUGH

(OR THE FIVE MINUTES BETWEEN 3:25 AND 3:30)

If she calls by four, I'll still have time to thaw out the veal, and we can have that with carrots, broccoli and potatoes.

If the phone rings in the next five minutes, it will be her, but if she rings after that, it will be Mum or Fabulous.

If Fabulous calls before I turn on the radio, Australia will be bowled out before tea, Warne won't have enough runs to play with, and the West Indies will win just after lunch on the last day.

If I turn on the radio and Steve Waugh is in, Australia will collapse and be all out before stumps, but if either of the not-out batsmen is 27, Australia will win.

If she calls after five, we'll just have to buy takeaway, because there's no point thawing out a good piece of veal and having it go to waste because she's late, or she's already eaten without having the courtesy to tell me.

If the repair people quote more than $120 for the VCR, I'll knock them back and get Fabulous to have a look at it, but if they say it's fucked, I'll write a letter to the manufacturer telling them that it's only six weeks out of warranty.

If I get through two more papers before three thirty-five, I'll check the scores, and if I turn on the radio and Steve

Waugh is already out, I'll turn off the radio and not listen again till after tea, but if I turn on the radio and Steve Waugh is in, but not on strike, I'll keep listening till tea or till Steve Waugh is out.

If the manufacturer refuses to come good, I'll threaten them with Consumer Affairs, or threaten to contact the Minister for Consumer Affairs.

If Steve Waugh is already out and I have to turn off the radio, I'll take a stroll down to the newsagent, and if the book is reviewed in *ABR*, or in one of the monthlies, Ian Healy will make fifty and Australia will win the Test, but if they win the Test on the back of Ian Healy's fifty, they'll lose the series.

If she calls after six, I'll tell her to bring home takeaway, that she can't expect me to cook for her if she never lets me know what she intends to do.

If the phone rings in the next thirty-five minutes, I won't answer it, unless it rings five times before four, in which case I'll answer the fifth call.

If I turn on the radio and Steve Waugh hits the first ball I hear described for four, a close relative will die before Christmas.

If Fabulous drops over before five, I'll tell him that she's been giving me the shits and I'm moving out.

If she comes in after seven and doesn't mention this bloke by name in the first five minutes, that'll mean she wants to fuck him.

If I ask her what this bloke means to her and she lies, or says that he doesn't mean anything to her, that'll mean she's been fucking him without telling me, but if she tells me that she's been fucking him but wants to stay here in the house, I'll tell her she can stay here so long as she never brings him to the house, but if she brings him to the house I'm going, because she can't expect me to stay if she can't respect my sensitivities.

If I turn on the radio and Steve Waugh gets out to the first ball I hear described, that'll mean she wants me to piss off.

If the repair people call to say that they can do the VCR for $120, but I'll have to wait another week for them to get in a part, that'll mean she wants me to stay.

If the phone rings in the next half hour, I'll only answer the third call, and if it's Fabulous or Mum, she won't come in tonight, and she won't call me.

If she comes back drunk and tells me that she's been out pissing-on with him, I'll tell her how I actually feel about her, that I've always loved her, even if she tries to make me shut up about it.

If I turn on the radio and Steve Waugh is still in but gets run out between tea and stumps, Australia will win the series.

If she actually comes home with him, if she brings him back here . . . if she actually brings him back here with her tonight, I don't know what I'll do.

CLOUDY DAYS
IN VELESK

To the best of my knowledge, no weather has been forecast for Velesk tomorrow. Nor has any weather been anticipated in Velesk these past eight years. For most people, Velesk is now no more than a quaint memory. More quaintness than memory. Can someone be said to remember the immaterial? Is it possible to retain the memory of an insinuated city? Maybe these are questions better left to philosophers and theologians. But I know that I am not alone in yearning for weather reports which offer metaphysical distraction.

I first heard about Velesk from my friend Christine. I was dubious initially, but Christine is a level-headed woman, not given to fantastic speculation. Eight years ago, she was teaching geography and politics at a prestigious girls' school, and she had already published scholarly articles on Australian foreign policy in the Asian region. Due to these interests, Christine made an effort to monitor international news broadcasts. She rarely missed the SBS World News in the evening. Following the local weather forecasts, SBS ran a summary of weather in major cities around the world. The international forecasts appeared as a graphic which detailed as many as sixteen cities, three or four of which were verbally highlighted by the newsreader during the ten seconds the graphic appeared on screen. One Thursday evening, eight years ago this week, Christine's attention was seized by the newsreader's reference to a city she had never heard of: 'Ten to twenty-one, and clear in Velesk.' Christine's eyes rushed to the graphic. Wedged between forecasts for Tel Aviv and Vienna was:

Velesk   Clear 10–21

Christine thought it odd that an unfamiliar city should be considered prominent enough to be included with New York, London, Mexico City, Buenos Aires, and Johannesburg in a list of major cities. She went to her comprehensive Gazetteer of the World, expecting that Velesk would turn out to be a heavily populated, politically insignificant city in the nether regions of Eurasia. She imagined that she would find Velesk in the backblocks of the former Soviet Union, a city of two or three million souls tucked away somewhere between Tadzhikstan and Kazakhstan. But neither her Gazetteer nor the Oxford Atlas made any mention of a city named Velesk.

The former Soviet states were highly volatile then, and it was far from unusual for cities to take on new names, or to revert to former names. Political allegiances shifted dramatically as states achieved independence, or sought to assert their independence from centralised regimes. So Christine was not surprised when her reference books let her down. She thought that the news department at SBS would be able to clarify the situation, but a frazzled producer told her she had no idea where Velesk was, and that she was uncertain how the city came to be mentioned on the newsreader's autocue, or the accompanying graphic. There had been no mention of Velesk being highlighted on the producer's running sheet. The news department suspected a practical joke, though they also thought that it might prove to be the result of a computer virus. A weather bulletin on the Internet had also mentioned the name Velesk, which was then, according to their sources, anticipating a clear day, with a maximum of twenty-one, following a minimum of ten.

By next morning, Christine had forgotten the episode. She didn't even think to mention it in the staffroom. But scanning a copy of *The Age* during her lunchbreak, she found among the brief weather forecasts for the major cities of the world— this time sandwiched between Valletta and Vienna:

Velesk   Clear 10–21

None of Christine's teaching colleagues had ever heard of Velesk. The head of the geography department suggested that Velesk was probably just a misprint for the Russian city of Volsk, a port on the Volga River. However, on that evening's SBS World Weather Outlook, following Toronto on the graphic listing of major cities, Christine was once again surprised to see:

Velesk   Cloudy 12–19

Christine soon realised that she was not alone in her curiosity. A small report on page six of the following day's *Age* indicated that readers had been calling the paper to glean some knowledge of Velesk. The newspaper's editorial staff had been unable to explain the sudden appearance of an unknown metropolis in international weather information. The author of the piece echoed the SBS suspicion of a computer virus, or even a hoax, and indicated that *The Age* would omit reference to Velesk in future forecasts until 'Velesk makes itself known to the geo-political community.' Nevertheless, on page 28 of the same edition of the paper, readers found exactly the same forecast that SBS had reported the previous evening:

Velesk   Cloudy 12–19

It should have already been clear to those interested in the matter that Velesk, having waited so long to present itself to the world, would not be easily disregarded.

A couple of days after that, at about the time Christine first contacted me, commercial news bulletins began to report the mysterious case of a persistently nonexistent city that seemed to be experiencing a succession of cloudy days. The puzzling appearance of Velesk in world weather forecasts had not been confined to SBS or *The Age*. Information services worldwide were reporting the receipt of these summary weather outlooks for a city no one knew anything about. Initially, these news agencies suspected a computer malfunction or a virus, but a still more curious phenomenon followed. The enigmatic Velesk seemed to resist any attempts to obliterate or ignore it. Television producers in Japan and Argentina declared an inability to correct any graphic or autocue reference which pertained to Velesk. References to Velesk would be deleted, only to reappear just as world weather information was being broadcast.

The tone of initial reports on the Velesk mystery was flippant. Cynical reporters treated the matter as a leg-pull, the technological equivalent of circles in cornfields. The news audience was expected to deduce that Velesk was a gremlin, or cybermutant. Attempts to solve the problem had somehow bred a form of treatment-resistant offspring. It says something for human need that usually ignored international weather forecasts so quickly became cult viewing. And the new cult was not let down:

Velesk   Cloudy 12–22

It wouldn't be entirely correct to say that the determination of a non-city to propel itself into existence seized my imagination. What really captured my imagination, and captured the imagination of others who knew my fiction—Christine among them—was how closely this peculiar eruption resembled my published fantasies. The mystery could so easily have been a story written by me. A tale of theories, speculations, false assumptions, and presumed conspiracies. So it wasn't a surprise when local literary critics voiced the opinion that this Velesk scenario *was* a story that I had manufactured.

These critics erred by overlooking a pertinent detail: Velesk was a global mystery, and my connections in the sphere of multimedia did not extend beyond Melbourne.

The Age published an article by the cultural studies guru

Nick Johnson which emphasised similarities between the appearance of Velesk and events depicted in my short story 'Transcendence'.

Though flattered to be thought capable of perpetrating a delicate hoax on such a large scale, my delight was tempered by several confusions which undermined Nick Johnson's argument.

To begin with, Johnson confused 'Transcendence' with another story in the same collection, 'Star Gazing'. In 'Star Gazing', the inhabitants of a large Melbourne-like city open their morning newspapers to find outrageously personalised and telling astrological predictions. These predictions are unique to each reader. The newspaper's management is at a loss to explain the appearance of so many different predictions within the same edition. Naturally, the editorial staff of their tabloid opposition insist that it's a dirty stunt, and are quick to make imputations about the mental stability of readers who claim that they are being addressed directly via astrological prediction.

As neither 'Transcendence' nor 'Star Gazing' were stories I wished to hang my literary hat on, I was slightly embarrassed to field enquiries from media enthused by the Johnson argument. Reporters asked whether I was solely responsible for the Veleskan microfiction, or whether I was part of an international plot. I stated my admiration for anyone who could have brought off such an ingenious hoax, if it was a hoax, and sought to assert my innocence. A dramatic change in the meteorological outlook supplied a convenient diversion:

Velesk   Rain 12–18

In the United States, two theories soon gained preeminence. The first argued that weather forecasts for Velesk were coded messages from aliens; the equivalent of saying, Watch This Space. The second theory argued an earthbound conspiracy. The forecasts could be read as a series of coded messages being transmitted either by a powerful international drug syndicate, a terrorist organisation, or a secret society flexing its muscles to demonstrate a new subversive potential.

Christine knew the mediocrity of my literary output sufficiently well to realise that Velesk, for all the sublime modesty of its existence, was bigger than anything I could imagine. When she saw that I had been dragged into the game, she dropped over with her latest researches.

At that stage, there had been something like nineteen separate weather forecasts for Velesk. Christine fed this information into her computer in the hope of obtaining a geographical fix on the city. Velesk seemed to have a temperate climate. By relating temperature-range and volatility to the one-word description, Christine's computer suggested autumn, which then implied that an earthly Velesk would have to be located in the northern hemisphere. Of course, the computer's deductions presumed that 'tomorrow' in Velesk coincided with a tomorrow somewhere on earth. Depending on the premises you operated with, the weather forecasts for Velesk were capable of confirming whatever you wanted to believe about practically anything:

Velesk   Clear 10–23

'Clear' suggested a visual depth of field, the opposite of murky. Were the good citizens of Velesk able to *see* their weather, to perceive atmospheric conditions in the way that we perceive them? And what could the degrees mean? In relative terms, a minimum temperature of ten could be unbearably cool, while a maximum of twenty-three might be hot enough to endanger the health of frail, elderly Veleskans.

Clear—Clear—Clear might have been the three oranges on a cosmic poker machine, the signal for an attack, or international political subversion. Cloudy, on the other hand, warned operatives to maintain their stealth. Nothing was concrete. Everything was possible.

A Hobart travel agent achieved notoriety by taking book-

ings for tours to Velesk, advising prospective clients that they
should pack to take account of all weather contingencies.

Velesk   Cloudy 10–21

Those who weren't terrified of imminent alien invasion
joked about the Veleskan obsession with the weather. People
made light about the drought in the capital, describing the
Veleskans sinking bores, and applying water restrictions. Just
two days of drizzle, and one day of rain in twenty-two. What
could 'Rain' mean to Veleskans? An intense continuous down-
pour, or periodic showers?

On day twenty-four, Christine had a letter published detail-
ing her view that Velesk was situated somewhere between
fifty to sixty degrees north of the equator. The city's weather
did not appear to be subject to temperature fluctuations
caused by proximity to an ocean, lending weight to her
argument that Velesk—whether it had a population of ten, or
ten million—was situated somewhere within a 300 kilometre
radius of Orsk in the former Soviet Union. The publication of
Christine's computer-fix on international news services led to
immediate rebuttal from scientists in Boston, who were 'practically certain' Velesk would be found somewhere between
Columbus, Ohio and Baltimore. By contrast, Italian scientists
insisted that they had all but fixed the coy metropolis in
Belgium.

The geographical 'fixes' inspired treasure seekers and
Doomsday cultists to descend upon the regions specified.
Some of these travellers said that they expected to find a
buried alien spacecraft, while others had their hearts set on
Noah's ark, or Nazi gold reserves. Others said that they
merely wanted to be on site, prepared to receive further
instruction.

Velesk   Clear 9–23

I particularly recall a senior NASA official who had his
employment terminated after stating categorically that the
forecasts represented a coded communiqué to an alien who

had been stranded on earth. The Velesk weather reports informed the alien of a newly arranged rendezvous with a spacecraft which would transport him back to his planet. On the same day, a prominent French intellectual asserted that the mystery had been fabricated by NASA as a means of securing a financial boost to the US space budget.

Velesk   Clear 10–21

Once dragged into the debate, my 'expert' views continued to be sought by television companies desperate to keep the game in motion. Television ratings figures were higher than they had been since the early days of colour television. The climate of heightened anxiety sparked a retailing boom. The public couldn't get enough Velesk. Any new observation, with just the slightest shift of emphasis, was apt to be seized upon, igniting a new outbreak of theories and counter-theories. My view was that people had been taking the matter too literally, or too metaphorically, and the truth lay somewhere in between these extreme depictions of Veleskan reality. The forecasts needed to be subjected to a more lateral analysis.

Velesk was a city which existed only through a capacity to project its future existence. Though we knew something about Veleskan expectations for the immediate meteorological future, we knew nothing about the accuracy of these forecasts, or how these anticipated futures came to merge with the present. We did not know what the weather had actually *been* in Velesk, or even whether it made sense to speak of Velesk existing in the present moment. I was convinced of the pointlessness of searching for Velesk as a geographical location. Our only knowledge of Velesk was as a temporal site, or projected site. Our failure to locate Velesk was a problem related to our conception of time.

If Velesk proved to be a city on a planet in a distant universe, it would make no sense to speak of a Veleskan tomorrow, or 'forecast', in the same way that we might speak of tomorrow in Paris. It is always problematic enough to speak of now, a *now* that exists simultaneously in both Melbourne and Gdansk, let alone drag the notion of an intergalactic *then* into the equation. The Veleskan forecasts were as much about the meaning and possibility of tomorrow as they were about a single, unambiguous tomorrow which would happen, inevitably, within the terms of tomorrow as we ordinarily understand it. For all we knew, these Veleskan tomorrows might have been ten days ago, or ten million years ago. To suggest that cunning Veleskans had specifically targeted this civilisation for the purposes of instruction, or even a practical joke, was just a little earthocentric. It was the psychological equivalent of the scientific thinking Galileo swept out the door.

Velesk   Rain 12–18

In an article published in *The Age*, I proposed two theories. The first argued that Velesk was indeed a city on earth, and that Veleskans had employed this nearly microscopic assertion of existence as a means to reach back to us from the future. The forecasts could then be seen as a form of quiet reassurance, a confirmation that there would be a future worth living. The future would be worth living because the people of the future cared enough about their fellow creatures to extend their care to the anxieties of their ancestors. The Veleskans of tomorrow didn't wish to unsettle us with powerful demonstrations, or to interfere with our situation in a way that might radically alter the course of history. The forecasts were a message left on an answering machine by Godot. There is a tomorrow worth waiting for. Things will become clearer.

Velesk   Clear 8–18

I favoured a second theory, not because it was more open to verification than any other, merely because it endorsed my own system of belief. Quite simply, I hold that time—by which I mean chronological time, the orderly succession of pasts, presents, and futures—is an illusion. I believe that all history belongs to a single, indivisible moment, a moment of pure finitude which is, paradoxically, pure infinitude. The eternal. Our sense of directed, or progressive movement through time, of one event causing or determining its successor, merely suggests the physical limit of our capacity to perceive, measure, and comprehend 'external' experience. Our sense of ordered succession through time only describes the extent of our power to engage with the universe, rather than indicate defining laws which pertain to the universe itself. All the events of time exist contemporaneously—the Battle of Agincourt alongside the crucifixion of Jesus Christ. Furthermore, all *possible* events, every possible course of history, exist within this single eternal moment. Our perception broadens only slightly to allow a hint of these parallel realities. Hence *déjà vu*. Hence Velesk. Cloudy, tantalising, erotic Velesk.

The beauty of these Veleskan theories and speculations was that none of them could be disproved. All were equally credible, equally incredible. The unfathomable city was mysteriously egalitarian in concept, and indiscriminately mysterious in practice. The thirty-fourth and final forecast read:

Velesk   Cloudy 12–19

When the forecasts ceased (except for fabrications and hoaxes soon proven to be such), the Doomsday crowd expected the worst. But the worst was nothing more than the absence of further information in an already information-saturated world. Psychiatrists complained about being expected to treat vast numbers of patients grieving this sudden loss of the beyond. In truth, these psychiatric opportunists were trying to encourage people to feel a loss of beyondness. Velesk had been excellent for business, and psychiatrists were among the people who felt its loss most fervently.

I watched the weather forecasts and waited. Everyone did for a time. But gradually we came to accept that Velesk had no further need of our attention. Or else, we had exhausted our need for Velesk. The enigmatic city became the lost city, a presumed-dead city whose death could not be verified. Or maybe Velesk has gone into hibernation, and is preparing to erupt back into existence like an inverted Pompeii.

Eight years can pass in a day. Strangeness, however extreme, manages to be assimilated, accommodated, or even forgotten. There will certainly be anniversary reflections on the curious phenomenon of Velesk, but these reflections will be of no different order to anniversary recollections of Jonestown, or the Moonlanding, or the Kennedy assassinations. Maybe I am wrong to believe that Velesk is stranger or more compelling than a maritime disaster, or Pol Pot. Strangeness is as relative as time.

I suppose that I should get together with Christine, to recall our brief moment in the spotlight, and old times in Velesk. Christine was right. Not even in my wildest imaginings could I have invented modest, weather-fixated Velesk. Only a true genius could give shape to its rare clouds, or describe the unique elusiveness of Veleskan tomorrows.

THE
IMPERMANENCE
OF THINGS

A person with an excellent memory and a powerful imagination has no excuse for being bored. When everything else fails, there is always time-travel. Life, as Kundera once put it so succinctly, is elsewhere.

A person with an excellent memory and a powerful imagination will enjoy imagining potential boredom situations, situations that challenge the power of memory and imagination to alleviate the onset of boredom. The greatest challenge for that person is to imagine the condition of boredom itself, without looking beyond to its alleviation, without unintentionally activating the means of alleviation. The time machine is always fuelled and ready for motion. The greatest threat to the imaginative, memory-retentive time-traveller comes not from an obstructed passage through time but the prospect of avalanche, the danger that one might be overwhelmed by the consciousness of time itself.

Anxiety is the mortal enemy of the time-traveller. A time-traveller can use memory to conjure pain so acute that the prospect or possibility of pain *is* real pain. The specific form of anxiety that plagues the time-traveller is not fear of a specific event, or an apprehensiveness related to pain or deprivation, but the elevated consciousness of compressed time. *Everything is now.* Within the machine, within the path of the machine's motion, everything is immediate.

* * *

45

If I do not remember being a passenger in a train delayed by a snowdrift outside Stockholm, I imagine the situation so vividly that it becomes indistinguishable from genuine memory, or the memory of a dream.

My fellow passengers groan when the Swedish conductor advises that we may be delayed for as much as eight or nine hours. They are unable to face the terrible prospect of being alone with themselves for even so short a time. Most of them will experience this delay not as a disruption to their journey, but as a disruption to the motion of the planet. They live for sensation, for a sense of motion or progress, if only for that most illusory progress, the sense of their orderly progression through time. Once denied sensation, once left at the mercy of their intellectual or emotional resources, they are at risk of perishing from boredom. But the time-traveller receives any delay or postponement as an opportunity. The delay is empty time in the form of a canvas waiting to be caked thick with coloured pigments.

To lust is also to list. When the definitive text is written on time-travellers, the author will note a common disposition to express intensity, or concentrated temporal engagement, in the form of lists. A time-traveller endeavours to control time by reordering it, by ridiculing the foolishness of perceived chronologies. Delayed by a snowdrift outside Stockholm, the time-traveller will happily open his or her suitcase to produce a notebook which owes its presence in the suitcase to exactly this contingency. An empty notebook is a list willing itself into existence.

In this snowdrift notebook, I have written, or imagine myself having written, that, as of March 25th, 1996, I am 13,079 days old, and that my most immediate desire is to compile a list of The 100 Happiest Days.

Even for a seasoned time-traveller, this is no small challenge. One's happiest moments do not necessarily belong to the happiest days. Nor do the happiest days automatically number among the most momentous, since the momentousness of an event does not always reveal itself at the moment of event but within consideration of the moment. Momentousness is apt to shift with reconsideration and redefinition.

Equally, the time-traveller plagued with an overdeveloped consciousness of time is more conscious than anyone that the perception of happiness will always be betrayed by a poignancy intrinsic to happiness. The very tenuousness of the happy moment implies the assertion of lost happiness. The list of The 100 Happiest Days will not simply be the reclamation of those periods of most insistent pleasure, but a list of one hundred lost happinesses. Not even the time-traveller's skill at making the absent immediate can distort or annihilate the consciousness that one is travelling through the Empire of Poignancy.

To merely transcribe the list of The 100 Happiest Days from the Swedish notebook I had in front of me, or imagine that I once had in front of me, would serve little purpose. My list is a long succession of dates. These dates are shuffled, crossed-out, and rearranged. Double-ended arrows indicate the shifts and replacements that I once believed ought to be made. Each date corresponds to a day that is luminous within my memory, or my imagined memory. An exact transcription of such a list would make as much sense as a move-by-move description of a chess match to someone unfamiliar with the rules of chess, the names of the chess pieces, or the abbreviations used to describe those moves.

For instance, June 28th, 1995, and May 28th, 1995 vie for the top position on my hierarchical list of happiest days. One is crossed out to be replaced by the other, only for a double-ended arrow to indicate the provisional reinstatement of June 28th as the ascendant day among those 13,079 days of variable happiness. (How do you compare an exquisitely happy day of little 'event' with an exquisite day full of happy events?)

No simple reading of my denotations will summon the *intensity* of my engagement in the process. In order to classify the happiness of a given day, you need to recover that happiness by re-experiencing it, to become as one with the temporal milieu; all the complex emotional, physical, and historical contexts which erupted into those experiences of pure, sustained happiness.

You might look at the date June 28th, 1995 and see it as nothing more than an arbitrary division of time within a logical continuum. If you accessed a newspaper library, you could list a number of more or less significant events which took place on that day, or were reported on that day, or were expected to occur on that day. Your own diary may well record an entry for June 28th, 1995 which details business meetings or phone calls or personal encounters, or even the result of a football match. (Highly unlikely, it was a Wednesday.) For the time-traveller, a date is more than an indicator of a sequence of points within so-called objective time or history; it is a doorway.

Still, my failure to tidy or finalise the list betrays an increasing sense of frustration that I had with this 100 Days of Happiness list, and that dissatisfaction, or carefully imagined dissatisfaction, must pertain to the use of dates as signifiers of happy days. My personal happiness, the purity or intensity of my emotional or sexual exhilaration, did not make that *date* happy. Any heightened consciousness of time, of the peculiarly fluid experience of time that comes with time-travel, only serves to accentuate discontent with these sign-posts to the illusory presence of objective time.

It is meaningless to speak of time divisible into equal segments, as if all encounters with time take place according to the same rules and the same understanding of the rules. It's not as if any of us inhabit the present for more than a moment, let alone inhabit the *same* present. The very dates which make an hierarchical list possible or coherent intrude upon the (inviolably subjective) happiness to which those dates are supposed to refer. It was the equivalent of having signed my happiest days over to a calendar manufacturer. My moments of indescribable joy may as well have been appended to a glossy colour shot of a cat, or Thomas Hardy's Dorset, or a naked female bodybuilder.

Examining this notebook of lists, I see that I abandoned, or imagine that I see abandoned, the precision of a hierarchy that was to be my list of The 100 Happiest Days. That list is set aside in favour of a non-hierarchical listing of happy moments. I might have imagined then, or imagine now, that such acts of recollection would constitute a more intellectual or goal-directed activity than time-travel ordinarily involves. Considering this second list from a distance, it appears to be unusually targeted. Yet, there is also a truth, a genuine immersion that makes the list transportive. It not only maps a specific journey through time which pertains to the original journey or imagined journey, it acts to redirect me through time on an unanticipated return journey.

* * *

To recover the moment just before the first kiss, when focus begins to soften and the background begins to swirl, when you might have heard an almost imperceptible crunching of cogs as time drew to a halt.

Those moments as a young child watching the opening credits of Disneyland *when you could actually believe that happiness was not an emotional condition but a place.*

The hot-pink kite ducking and diving against the blue of an immeasurably blue sky.

Those moments when time was on the verge of bursting at the seams, when the regulation hour after dinner had passed, when the glare was so intense that you could barely open your eyes, the sand so hot beneath your feet that you had to run, the parched air full of salt and rotten seaweed and squealing children's voices, when there was no more exciting prospect in the world than the sensation of thrusting your head through the breaking waves, long locks of salty wet hair clinging to the back of your neck.

Moments when reality bewilders desire; Catherine O'Shaunessy enters the crowded lecture theatre and appears to be searching for someone, and you are astonished to realise that the history student she is searching for among all these history students is you.

Always those moments near the completion of an ordeal that you'd been dreading for months in advance—an examination, or a public speech, or a task which threatened to expose your inadequacy—when you realise the worst is over, and that soon you'll be in a hot bath, or sipping a glass of red wine, and the dark clouds over your appointment diary will have vanished.

Those time-stretched, slow-motion moments when all your despair at global conflict and famine is erased by the half-forward in the red and black guernsey who snatches the ball off the top of the pack and storms into goal, his fist punching the air even before the ball clears the umpire's head, when you feel a seizure in that place in your chest where coronary occlusion is indistinguishable from ecstasy.

In the train to Sandringham, reading Gogol's Dead Souls, *where in spite of your acute self-consciousness you begin to laugh hysterically, and just for once you couldn't give a fuck if everyone looks at you.*

And those moments in the car with your high school friends when it is unquestionable that you've landed among the most brilliant, exuberant group of people on earth, and you can switch on the car radio confident that the first song you hear will be your favourite song.

That feeling when it all clicks, when everything falls into place perfectly, and you see, you know, exactly what the author was getting at and why things were arranged in a certain order, when you appreciate the possibility of an essential order.

That moment when, after weeks of having photographs taken, arranging to have the mail redirected, repeated visits to the bank, calls to the travel agent, arranging someone to mind the dog, collecting the passport, doing financial calculations, finalising hotel arrangements, buying the new suitcase, visiting the old relatives who might die in your absence, having injections, attending farewell parties, making checklists, packing, repacking, redrafting the will, booking the taxi, queuing at the check-in, and bundling your luggage into the overhead locker . . . That precise, perfect moment when your arse hits the seat and you can begin to contemplate the possibility of a journey which might be more pleasure than ordeal.

* * *

Did I ever intend to make a list of one hundred of these moments, or a totally comprehensive list? . . .

Something is seizing me. We passengers on the train delayed by a snowdrift somewhere between Stockholm and the ferry to Denmark are advised that we will now be transferred onto a series of coaches. *I remember this now.* If I recall this coach transfer, I recall it as a time-traveller who has found his re-entry point in the form of a ridiculous, minimalist German pop song, *Da Da Da*, that an old lady on the coach insists we all sing along to. I am singing. I can hear my slightly flat, but not unenthusiastic voice among the ragtag choir of voices. This is a moment reclaimed from time in its entirety. Should I classify it according to a happiness ratio or expectation? I am in a coach driving along a highway somewhere in Sweden. It is snowing, and I am singing *Da Da Da*. Inside my suitcase is a list of happiest moments that might yet become more poignant through my failure to complete it. Someone passes a Danish pastry to me. I am singing *Da Da Da*. If it was in my power to take you with me, to share that pastry with you, I would. But you have no place in this journey because your notion of happiness, your notion of the possibility of happiness, does not depend on you being there. And that man with the raucous Australian voice two or three seats behind me. I remember him now. Steve Hair, a roadtrain driver from Katherine in the Northern Territory. Half-man, half-amphetamine. Steve is the one who will wake me from a deep sleep inside a warm railway carriage aboard the ferry to Denmark. He will pick me up and carry me up to the deck so that I can feel the snowflakes on my cheek. 'Snow! Isn't it fuckin' great? . . . Mate, we're in Scandinavia, and it's fuckin' snowing!' The raucous voice several seats behind me belongs to a man who will introduce himself to me as Steve Hair. I am on a coach driving along a frozen highway in Sweden. I am singing *Da Da Da*. I am travelling through time, deep into the Empire of Impermanence. I will never be bored.

GAVIN'S METHOD

Though most insults lose their impact through overuse, one or two vulgarities still manage to deliver, and we have a responsibility to be careful when using them. Terms like dag and dickhead have become endearments, but you can still trigger a brawl by calling someone a deadshit or a fuckwit. I mention this only to assure you that I have taken full account of my responsibilities to the language before making the following declaration: Gavin McGibbon is a turd.

* * *

You won't remember my name, but you may remember me as the so-called 'Fork Man'. I was a human interest story, the unlikely survivor of the flash floods at Narraya.

The whole thing was incredibly dumb. I didn't know that part of the country at all. The river rose so quickly that there was no time to get away, not even to climb back up to the main road. I remember being swept along by a wall of water, powerless in the current. I can't remember seeing the tree, so maybe I smashed against the trunk. I must have grabbed hold of it instinctively. I don't remember climbing to the knotted branch. Maybe I just rose with the level of the water. But I felt safe when I was there in the fork, even when the water was tugging at my knees. I felt confident that if I stayed there in the fork, everything would be all right. When the flood receded after a day or so, I was ten metres up with no way of getting down. I had the idea that I was in the fork six or seven days at most, and didn't believe the rescuers when they told me it was twelve. I'd been thinking about things, daydreaming, having quite a good time. The more thirsty and hungry I got, the weirder the dreams.

I thought it must have been the weird dreams and hallucinations that interested the television people. Well, who knows what I was thinking? I behaved like an idiot. Vivien Johnson told me that they wanted to make a film of my time up the tree, and that it was going to be like Beckett, Australian Beckett. Even after they'd paid me the twenty thousand, and their researcher spent just an hour chatting on the phone, I still believed they were interested in my experiences and that the film was going to be arty and challenging like Beckett.

* * *

The agreement I signed was seven pages long. I'm an intelligent person, and I've read plenty of documents, but most of the clauses and subclauses in this contract meant nothing to me. I should have asked for clarification. I suppose that I expect people to act in good faith. I trusted that I was dealing with people who wouldn't exploit the ambiguities of an oddly phrased agreement.

One of the stipulations I hadn't understood was that I would be expected to fully cooperate with preproduction research. I took that to mean that I would be required to offer what help was necessary to the production of the script. As it happened, I never even met the scriptwriter. But Vivien Johnson reiterated this full cooperation clause when she informed me that Gavin McGibbon was going to spend a week living with me. She said Gavin McGibbon would be playing my part in the film, and he needed to observe me at close range so that he could get into the character.

* * *

Gavin is taller than I am. Quite a bit taller, and much more muscular. He'd spent a lot of time in the gym. I couldn't think of one respect in which Gavin and I were alike. And when his name was first mentioned, I hadn't even heard of him. The producers told me that he was a highly respected dramatic actor, that he'd been nominated for a Logie. Critics would have told me that Gavin had been the heart-throb in two early-evening soaps. When I mentioned his name to friends who had seen him perform, they said, Oh . . . he's the last person I would have expected.

When I spoke to Gavin on the phone, I warned him about the lack of room in my flat, and he said that he didn't need much room. He said that I'd hardly notice him. He arrived at the front door with just two suitcases, video equipment, a full length mirror, and an exercise bike.

Gavin told me that he was excited to meet me. He said that getting this role, playing me in the telemovie, was going to be his big break. He told me that when he read the script, he thought the part had been written for him.

* * *

Say that again.
    Say *what* again?
    What you just said . . .
    Why?
    It's really interesting the way you crush your vowels. It's something to do with the positioning of your tongue.

* * *

Even when I cooked for both of us, Gavin never ate with me. At least, not in the usual sense of eating *with* someone. He video-taped me eating. After I'd eaten, Gavin sat down in front of the monitor and tried to mimic the way that I had eaten. Gavin told me that because of his training at the Institute of Dramatic Art, he would only take a day or two to have my eating habits down pat.

But Gavin, you're missing the point. I didn't eat anything while I was up the tree. I practically starved to death. The whole thing about my story is that I didn't eat.

But you eat in the flashbacks. You remember every meal you've ever eaten in perfect detail . . . Besides, I'm not trying to mimic you. This is about entering your psyche. By the end of this week, you should be able to confront me with an experience that you've never had to confront, and I'll handle it exactly the same way that you would.

That's great. Just now, I'm confronted with washing your dishes, which is something that I've never encountered before. How do you think I should handle it?

My money says you'll get angry, and that's good. I need to see what you're like when you're passionate.

* * *

I didn't like the way Harriet was so excited about meeting Gavin. And she shouldn't have said that Gavin McGibbon was too much of a hunk to play my part. When I told Harriet that Gavin was just a dumb soapie star pretending to be Robert de Niro, she said that I was a cultural snob. What could be dumber than getting caught ten metres up a tree for twelve days? She said that the hardest thing for Gavin would be to convince the audience that an intelligent man wouldn't have found some way to get down.

When Gavin told me that he would like to meet Janine, that he would need to see how Janine and I interacted, I couldn't think what he meant. Then I realised that the script-writer must have turned Harriet into Janine. I couldn't wait to phone Harriet to tell her that her hunk Gavin was now making a film about a stranded man who spends two weeks fantasising about the terribly desirable Janine.

* * *

If I walked down the street to get a paper, Gavin walked with me, trying to copy the way I walk. I noticed him getting rounder at the shoulders, and beginning to slouch. I tried to fill out my chest and press my shoulders back, but I couldn't sustain it.

People recognised Gavin in the street and spoke to him, and he would reply as he imagined I would reply, an embarrassed smile and a mumbled greeting, with eyes turned downward.

I could have said, For Chrissake, Gavin, cut it out, it's giving me the shits, but Gavin would have looked at me with sponge-eyes and committed my anger to memory.

One time, I came out of the shower to find him sitting on the couch next to Harriet, and he was asking her if she could remember the first time we kissed, and she told him that she hadn't really enjoyed it, because when I stuck my tongue in, it tasted of onion.

She'd always told me that it was the most perfect kiss she'd ever had.

* * *

You don't seem to like your parents very much.

Whaddaya mean? I love my parents.

The way you speak to them on the phone. It's like a business call.

We're very reserved people. It doesn't mean that we don't love each other.

59

But you know that they don't approve of Janine.

Harriet! . . . My parents love Harriet. My parents think that Harriet's great.

Your mother told you that she was just a tart.

She *what*? Who told you that? Did Harriet tell you that? . . . It's bullshit! My mother's never said that. She would never say anything like that.

No? What about when you told your mother about the abortion?

The *what*? What fucking abortion? Harriet's never had an abortion, and if she'd had an abortion, I certainly wouldn't tell my mother about it . . . Where the fuck have you been getting this crap?

* * *

Gavin told me that he hadn't brought the script with him because he had already committed it to memory. Among the things Gavin didn't tell me was that lawyers had instructed him not to show me the script or to divulge details of the script. When Gavin told me that he thought the script had been written for him, he neglected to mention that he'd paid someone to write it for him. Gavin never once let on that he was the film's executive producer.

* * *

You don't eat very well, do you?

Gavin, fuck off!

You need more fruit, more fibre . . .

Gavin!

And you should have your eyes tested. Have you ever noticed the way that you squint?

* * *

Twenty-thousand dollars sounds like a lot of money. You can think of a lot of things that you can do with twenty-thousand dollars. If someone offers you twenty-thousand dollars and they don't seem to be asking for much in return, you are inclined to accept their offer. But there are circumstances in which twenty-thousand dollars doesn't seem like a lot of money, and in those circumstances you begin to question the kind of things that can be given monetary value, and the highly relative meaning of a term like 'lot'. It's possible for a lot to be a lot and still not be nearly enough.

* * *

Gavin began to answer the phone as me, saying that it was me, and conduct conversations where he would make decisions and offer opinions on my behalf. That didn't matter so much if he was speaking with someone who had called to speak to him, or to the producers of the telemovie, but I was infuriated to find him arranging dinner with Harriet and asking if Gavin could come along.

Gavin, if you want to have dinner with my girlfriend, you ask her out as Gavin, but don't ask her out as me. And don't have me asking if you can tag along, because I wouldn't want you to be there, all right?

It's O.K. She didn't know that it wasn't you.

Bullshit!

She thought it was you. I've mastered the way that you talk. I've locked-in to the negative way you think. Harriet thought it was you. And she sounded like she was really keen for Gavin to come along.

Look, if you and Harriet want to fuck, you should fuck, but leave me out of it.

Well, I don't think that I could . . . I mean, I'd need to watch the two of you fucking before I could fuck her the way you would.

61

Gavin . . . I wasn't serious.

But it would help. I think it's a good idea.

* * *

I told Gavin that my innermost fears were private, that they were my business.

No, your fears are my business . . . That's if you want to see yourself portrayed honestly. Maybe you're not prepared for that.

Gavin, I don't mean to be hurtful or negative, but you *can't* do it. You're nothing like me. You're a talentless moron.

You're beginning to see yourself through me.

Bullshit!

And you're scared of confronting things that have always terrified you . . .

Gavin . . .

When you were a kid, you were disgusted by handicapped people, weren't you? And that old coat of yours, you think that wearing it keeps you safe from bad people and acts of God . . .

Fuck off!

* * *

It was later, weeks later, that Harriet told me she and Gavin had slept together. A strange moment. I had expected to be homicidal or suicidal if I ever discovered that Harriet had been unfaithful. I was surprised to find myself numb. It was a numbness that I took for indifference, and Harriet saw it that way too, turning on me, saying that it proved I never really loved her. She said that I was incapable of real love, because I was unable to confront my deepest fears.

Hey, wait a second. It was you who slept with that big dumb fuck!

It was no big deal. I don't care about Gavin. He said it would help him to understand you better if we slept together, and I thought that it might help me to understand you better.

How very understanding! It must have been a glorious therapeutic experience for both of you!

As a matter of fact, I didn't enjoy it. He gave a very technical performance . . .

You let Gavin fuck you!

No, I didn't. I wish that I had let Gavin fuck me. I wish that Gavin had wanted to be Gavin as he fucked me. As it was, I couldn't really tell the difference.

* * *

I've heard a lot of stories told—maybe they're apocryphal, I don't know—about the American actor Dennis Hopper coming out to Australia to play the bushranger, Mad Dog Morgan. Hopper was a student of 'the method', and got into a role by trying to become the person he was playing. He would stay in character even when he wasn't on set. Anyway, the stories have it that bushranger Dennis ran amok through southern New South Wales, holding up tourist buses at gunpoint. The producers had permanent brainache trying to keep Dennis out of gaol.

Method actors tend to have a highly underdeveloped sense of irony, and this deficiency allows them to plough on regardless. When I found Gavin practising my signature in my chequebook, he wasn't even embarrassed.

It's close, but I haven't quite got it. You press so hard.

That's it, Gavin, you've gone too fucking far!

Hey, do that again, the thing you just did with your lip . . .

I'm gathering up all your stuff, and I'm dumping it out on the street.

It's like a twitch . . . I can use that.

63

Gavin, I'm gathering up all your stuff, and I'm dumping it out on the street.

This might be a good time for you to hit me. I think that you want to.

I moved toward the guest bedroom, doing my very best to stay calm. Gavin, I'm dumping your stuff out on the street.

Gavin looked at me, and repeated what I'd said with exactly the same intonations. Then he tried it again, this time slightly altering his emphasis on the word 'dumping'.

Bit by bit, I gathered up Gavin's stuff and dumped it out on the street.

* * *

I once spent twelve days sitting in the fork of a tree, frightened that I would starve to death, remembering all the things that had ever happened to me, sucking rainwater off gumleaves, fantasising about Harriet, and rehearsing the wonderful reunions that would follow my rescue. Reality and dream and fear and hallucination all meshed together like a perfect work of art. My sister Maggie said Gavin was the price I had to pay for not treasuring the integrity of a unique experience. Maggie told me I lacked strength of character.

* * *

Harriet was invited to the special preview screening, but she'd already moved to Canberra. And I would have declined the invitation too, if the producers hadn't sent the limousine to fetch me. I tried to avoid Gavin, and the publicist berated me for refusing to have my photograph taken with him. It made no difference. They took photos of us individually, then tricked them together, so the entertainment magazines could feature photographs of Gavin and me with our arms around each other at the preview of 'the film tipped to make Gavin McGibbon a superstar'.

Gavin was already behaving like a superstar. He arrived with his glamorous new girlfriend, Liz Mitchell, who, as coincidence had it, was the film's scriptwriter. Liz told television reporters she always had it in the back of her mind that she would do something with Gavin.

I drank too much wine, and sat with my family, trying to conceal my despair as the ninety-five minute travesty flickered away on the big screen . . . The great imbecile camped in the fork of a tree, the great turd's head flooding with puerile thoughts I'd never had, nourishing himself with the memory of sentimental moments I'd never experienced.

When the film ended, there was a prolonged silence. Then, unaccountably, an intense volley of applause. I was staggered. How could people embrace this tripe? Even the toughest critics were on their feet screaming for Gavin, and Gavin rose to acknowledge them with a wave and a smile. I heard a voice from behind me say, This will be the making of him. He could be anything that boy.

When the applause died down, my mother turned to me and said she was sorry they'd changed my story and made such an awful movie.

It's all cliché, I said. It's total crap.

Yes. But he was wonderful.

Who was?

Gavin . . . He had you down pat. Even the twitch . . . He was the dead spit.

It's funny. I'd often used that phrase, but I'd never really thought about it, where it comes from, and what it actually means. Of course, Mum's use of the dead spit, to suggest indistinguishability, was treacherous and inappropriate, the exact opposite of what I thought. But I liked it anyway, and decided that I'd use it myself . . . The dead spit. Yes, Gavin was the dead spit.

PACKING DEATH

If meaning resides in the presumption
of finality, in the certainty of death,
what meaning remains when death
itself is meaningless? Better not to
speak of the significance of one's
passing, post-modern death is chic.
Chic is death.

Kohji Morimoto, *The Annotated Approximation of Death*

1. Retractions

To judge from the lip-sized indentations on his cheek, Robert
had been kissed to death by an angel. Catherine thought it
would have suited Robert to be seen in the company of angels.
He loved to make an impression, and even in this posthumous
display, Robert exhibited a certain style, his aberrant facial
recesses handsomely suited to aberrant times. This elegance
notwithstanding, a death certificate had to be written. In the
absence of a scientific reason to explain why Robert's heart
had given out, the coroner would once again be called upon
to redefine her understanding of death.

The boundaries of death had been contracting for many
months in these suburbs, and to account for this trend in her

certifications Catherine had developed an increasingly mysti-
cal code of classification: Death from Lack of Event, Death
from Retraction of Life, Death from Elaborate Inactivity.

Catherine had known Robert once. He was an opportunist
who would squeeze through narrow gaps at official functions
to fill a vacant glance with his vain self-assurance. Yes, she
had known Robert. When he was spent, his reproductive
reflex folded away like a well-oiled extension ladder. Now
Robert was entirely spent; Dead, as Catherine recorded,
through Want of Opportunity to Live.

The coroner's art in these times is to see a possible fluidity
in inertia. A practised eye, Professor Kenyon once argued, will
perceive cessation of desire as clearly as the stilled circulation
of blood.

There were still many in the suburbs who confused so-
called morbid achievement with style because of its fashionable associations—all the most fashionable people were dying.
Fashion-conscious herself, Catherine had been chosen to head
the Pathological Anomalies Commission. Under her guidance
the administration sought to warn the suburbs against the
Death Cult, and their slavish adherence to trend. Desire is a
fierce contagion, Catherine told her colleagues. Desire draws
nourishment from its own vacuity.

In recent weeks Catherine had observed that her grip on
surgical instruments would alter to facilitate the need for impre-
cise findings, and she marvelled at her own capacity to adapt
to circumstance. That said, she never enjoyed autopsying
acquaintances. Robert, though technically excellent in death,
had disturbed her customary delight in post-mortem examination. Having stripped off her gloves, Catherine looked once
again at Robert's corpse, and the pregnant stillness of it made
her think of Morimoto's legendary performance in *The Approximation of Death*. Taking account of this, Catherine altered her
classification to read, 'Death through Static Insistence'.

Catherine put aside her implements, and stretched out a sheet to veil Robert's indifference to life. She was hungry. With the Great Parade imminent, and Melbourne so much under the sway of The Cult, Catherine would need to fuel her resolve. All too soon the suburbs would be bursting with innovative mortality. In time, this new vogue might exhaust even Catherine's capacity to make and remake the poetry of death.

> I'm telling you, we're in a Peter Pan
> situation. You've gotta believe in life
> after death, otherwise . . . Otherwise,
> Melbourne's gonna disappear.
>
> Richard Thompson, *Death Warmed Up*

2. Death Warmed Up

'The people of supposedly quainter times knew better than to tempt fate. If required to mention death or the dead in passing, they would cross themselves, or speak in lowered tones. No-one would have joked about a circumstance, however unlikely, that might lead a person to commit suicide. To joke about death was to make an enemy of The Vast Net.

Nowadays the queues outside Melbourne's death clubs are so long that the crowds mingle and intersect, one group to see the Suicide Comics from New York, another to see Berlin's Joke Immolators. By far the longest queue is to see the local boy, Richard Thompson, in his one-man show, *Death Warmed Up*. The crowd with the black tulip lipstick mingles with the Blackhoods. When you consider the price of admission, it's a wonder that so many manage to embrace the death vogue so enthusiastically. Still, the death clubs are cheaper than a tour of the cemetery or an exhibition at the morgue, and just a small fraction of the cost of Designer Death.

Buzzed-out on morbid tribulations, a suicide club patron shoves through the crowd, shouting crazily as he pushes aside two plain-clothes police officers, "So fuckin' profane! The dross who dress best dress to die!"

The police don't contest this. No-one here in this crowd, at this time, would contest what he says. The way things are, people want to believe that anyone can die a significant death, that even the prohibitive costs can be circumvented with panache, or 'dying grace', as the journalists refer to it.

Richard Thompson never imagined that he had grace of any kind. If you ask him about his new fame, he says that it was a matter of being in the right place to latch onto the breaking wave. His good fortune is to be a morbid obsessive at a time when morbid obsession signifies cultural superiority. As he tells his audience now, there's too much money to be made articulating despair and fuelling the spirit of innovative death for him to seriously consider killing himself. "But that only makes it more fun to *imagine* killing myself."

Away from the theatre Richard Thompson is a nervous, diffident man. He will tell you that he still doesn't know what his audience expects from him. His two-hour show is essentially formless, his anecdotes more painful than funny, but his half-mumbled, self-pitying observations are met with roars of approval. Thompson speculates that he has somehow come to embody living death, the life that celebrates its antithesis.

Only by this kind of iconographic theory can Richard explain why tourists crowd into Melbourne, why a beautiful city surrounded by gardens should have attained the status of an international Death Capital.

In the streets of the city's central business district, tourists stand above the corpses to photograph them. They ask friends and locals to photograph them with the dead.

"Heck, no-one ever died like that in Arkansas," enthuses the man in the baseball cap as he replaces the film in his Nikon. "The dead folks here, it's not like they die . . . they just seem to forget what's been keeping them alive." He drops onto his haunches so that he can photograph the bluish young woman as a blowfly enters her nostril.

Down the road, Alice and Ingrid have spent thirty-six hours in the queue for *Death Warmed Up*. Just fifteen, they find death attractive, but they can't afford a trendy demise. "You'd be letting your friends down if you died a stupid death," Alice says. "They'd be ashamed to visit you at the morgue. God, imagine if you didn't get an inquest!"

The girls hold copies of Richard Thompson's records and videos, hoping to have them signed. Ingrid is a true believer. "Our parents say that he fakes it for money, but you just can't fake that sort of depression. He wants to die. I'm sure that he would arrange for Designer Death if he wasn't such a coward."

"It's being a coward that makes him so cute," Alice adds.

Richard Thompson met Catherine O'Shaunessy several months before she was appointed head of the Pathological Anomalies Commission. Catherine was just a run-of-the-mill coroner then. Now they are Melbourne's most celebrated couple. In one of his monologues, Richard says that he first met Catherine by approaching her as she stood beside an ice-cream van. "I said, Hey, what's that perfume you're wearing? . . . Formaldehyde! And she said, Yes, as a matter of fact, it is."

Catherine tells a different version, that the pair met in the morgue when Richard was identifying a friend. "I didn't know about the stage business. I never have time to read or watch television. I was staggered by him. He was white and lifeless looking. I just saw him as someone with an incredible morbid potential."

When he dies, Richard has asked that Catherine record on his certificate, "Death as the perfect realisation of his morbid potential".

She is blonde with rounded shoulders and a slight lisp, naturally vivacious. They are an odd couple who would attract

73

attention irrespective of their fame. Before the two took out a court order, tour buses used to stop outside the Hampton apartment where they live with Lucy, Catherine's daughter from a previous marriage.

Souvenir hunters strip away the blue PAC transfers from the doors of Catherine's government car. Several people have chosen to die in their front garden, as a tribute, so the notes say.

You see from the look in Catherine's eyes that it can get too much for her sometimes. "Bodies at work, bodies by the roadside as I drive to work, bodies in the garden at home." She would like you to believe that this tiredness is itself a performance—how could anyone grow tired of death?—and that she is *simpatico* with modern death-styles, but you don't feel convinced. In the corner of her living room, daughter Lucy is rehearsing Lewis Carroll:

Twas brillig, and the slithy toves
Did gyre and gimble in the wabe;
All mimsy were the borogoves,
And the mome raths outgrabe.

There is something decidedly old-fashioned about death's most fashionable family.

As I accompany Richard on his way to the theatre, he confesses to being a nervous driver, and takes a roundabout route in order to avoid tram lines. His shoulders tense as he squeezes the steering wheel. Catherine, who knows all the puns, would say that he hangs on like grim death.

Driving through Armadale we observe a group of private-school children trying, but failing, to distinguish themselves in death. The poignancy of this leads me to ask Richard whether he ever feels disenchanted with his part in the new scheme of things.

"When I was at school, we had a football coach who was very big on macho. He couldn't tolerate us being wimps, so he was always rabbiting on about how a coward dies a thousand deaths, a hero dies but one. Of course, the message was that we should aspire to heroism. But when I thought about it, there was something wrong with the logic. It was years after school that it struck me . . . If a coward dies a thousand times, and a hero dies but once, then a coward must be a thousand times more heroic than a hero. It was a big discovery."

"So, do you think of yourself as a coward or a hero?"

"I think of myself as a Melburnian."

Extracted from Carlotta Valdes, *The Death Throes of Modern Capitalism*

> Despise the cretins who expect to *find* meaning. Then string up the Gallic collaborators who would have you believe that meaning is infinitely elusive, so that they might confuse the distinction between resistance and collaboration . . . Just cut the crap and cash your pay-cheques. Dare to be definite. Your actions will hierarchize time. Things must be *made to mean*.

Kohji Morimoto, *Approximate or Perish*

3. Love is Colder than Death

Only when she was driving did Catherine have time to herself. In the car she could shut out the February heat, the stench of decay, and the strain of days spent lugging dead weight. Behind her tinted windscreen the suburbs were all passionate shades of green, gold, and blue, and it was still possible to believe that her city was a place of beauty.

But sometimes the tensions of her day could not be shut out. Twice a month, Catherine, as Head of the Pathological

Anomalies Commission, met with a deputation from the Natural Death Collective, a group fundamentally opposed to the PAC mandate. Though some friction was inevitable, this afternoon's meeting had particularly infuriated Catherine, when distraction was the thing she could least afford. She had been entrusted to make sense of things, to defend logic and coherence by redefining the principles of logic where the need arose. If she lost sight of her objective, took her eyes off the ball for just a moment, she could be overwhelmed by The Cult.

Catherine was well acquainted with the NDC people and their specific factional interests. It was customary for the Funeral Cosmeticians to accuse Catherine's staff of unnecessary mutilation. Likewise, the Narcoleptics could be expected to complain that PAC inquests ignored the statutory cooling-off period which applied to the autopsy of registered narcoleptics. What Catherine hadn't expected was a shift to a more personal line of attack.

In previous meetings Father Maguire had demonstrated that he was a mystery merchant of the old school. Now Maguire wanted to argue that the Commission's determination not to classify Cult Death as suicide devalued life, and left Catherine open to the charge that she was a stooge of government: 'a government already stooge to the Designer Death Corporation of Atlanta'.

According to the cleric's reasoning, hundreds of people committing suicide would signify social collapse and official incompetence, so it was crucial for this administration that 'morbid exuberance' be accepted as a mark of Melbourne's sophisticated internationalism. In turn, this bizarre form of liberal self-expression fed back into the politicians' pockets by virtue of personal holdings in Designer Death.

Though Catherine did not claim to be ignorant of these rumours—Melbourne was held together by elaborate works of fantasy—she insisted that no politician would dare to interfere with her autonomy at the PAC. Government was depending on her Commission to reinvigorate the notion of meaningful society.

But Catherine's defence was of no interest to them. It transpired that Maguire's accusations were only a prelude to the deputation's main assault.

As they returned from a coffee break, Maguire told Catherine that he would demand her resignation. If she did not resign, the NDC would be compelled to reveal that the independence of her Commission had been compromised by her relationship with Richard Thompson. Maguire's face reddened as he led the interrogation.

Is it, or is it not the case that your de facto intends to sign a multi-million dollar contract to endorse Designer Death?

I know nothing about any contract, Catherine told them, and I *would* know if there was a contract. What's more, if I were you, I'd be very careful about making that kind of accusation in public.

* * *

As she sat in a long queue of motionless traffic, Catherine mulled over this last statement about the need to be extremely careful, and she began to question just how careful she had been in becoming involved with Richard. What did she know about him? She could be certain that he was good with Lucy, that he was justly famous for being a morose coward, and that he sometimes made her feel like a necrophiliac when they made love. Was any of that enough to be sure that he wouldn't compromise her, that he wouldn't jeopardise her career?

When Lucy's father, Martin, was appointed Professor of Physiology at NYU, he had expected that Catherine and Lucy would follow him to New York. And Catherine would have followed Martin, if he hadn't presumed that she would. With Richard it had never been so complicated. At least, it hadn't seemed complicated. Maybe the casual independence they affected only worked because they hadn't yet had cause to define what was essential to them.

When Catherine arrived home there was no sign of Alice's blue Mazda. Hiring a nanny had been meant to ensure that Lucy wouldn't be left to her own devices. While Alice minded Lucy, Catherine could work late at the morgue, and Richard was free to come and go from the theatre. So it surprised Catherine to find her daughter alone, sprawled in front of the television, munching from a tall stack of Vegemite toast.

Where's Alice?

Dicky said that she could go home.

Where's Richard?

Taking a nap.

That'd be right.

Ignoring the stink of recently burnt toast, Catherine checked her answering service, noting in her diary the location of corpses that she would arrange to have examined. There was a message from the Premier's office, asking her to call urgently, and there was a further message for Richard from an odd-sounding man, George someone, who advised that he would call back to confirm flight details and accommodation arrangements.

Catherine sat motionless next to the phone for a moment. Had George spoken with a southern accent? The noise from the television began to gnaw at her, and she called out to Lucy.

Luce, haven't you got homework to do?

I've done it, she said. It's on the dining-room table.

On the dining-room table, Catherine found a large sheet of project paper, which featured a pastiche of photographs and Lucy's stylish, if difficult handwriting. Typically, she had headed the project in bold red texta: *Corpus Delectable: Melbourne's Coolest Cadavers*.

Each photograph referred to a recently dead teenage celebrity, among them Christine Andrews, the Olympic swimmer, Jason Williamson, the champion footballer, and Elizabeth Phillips, guitarist and songwriter with the band Approximate Life. All had been autopsied and certified by Catherine. Now, as she looked at their faces, and the grimness which belied their great promise, she knew that The Cult masked a failure that was bigger than the fate of individuals, that what it hid was a collective failure of imagination.

It's great, she called to Lucy. Excellent work.

It was then that Catherine noticed a letter sitting on the corner of the sideboard, a thickly packed envelope that carried three American stamps and the insignia of the Designer Death Corporation.

* * *

Sleeping naked, Richard's body was an unimpressive thing. He was flabby, and the coarse mat of hair on his chest spread to ugly tufts on his shoulders. Richard often said that sleeping on his back inspired lascivious dreams, but more significantly, from Catherine's point of view, it made him snore, and a gaping mouth gave Richard's face the hint of imbecility.

Pity his fans never see this, Catherine thought.

Catherine concentrated her gaze. She anticipated that Richard's flesh would be cool to her touch—blood seldom heated his extremities—but now she feared the things that she might never know about him. As a professional, it was her responsibility to make final determinations, to be definite above all else. If this extracurricular plan was to be carried out, she would need to act resolutely, to fetch her instruments and set to work. Whether or not Richard woke would be of no consequence. His eyes would open just long enough to register a final shock as she pushed the scalpel blade through his throat.

* * *

Much later, Catherine would refer to the hesitation that saved Richard as belief, though she never made it clear what it was that she had chosen to believe in: Richard, Richard's loyalty, or some abstract conviction about belief itself. Nor did she indicate whether she thought this belief justified by subsequent events.

When questioned about her professional integrity, or the radical shifts in zeal that marked her career, Catherine liked to quote something that her friend Rosi had said of Sartre, that he was to be most admired for having the courage of his contradictions.

Had it been courage or contradiction that spared Richard?

Catherine would smile broadly as she recalled the near-murder.

Look, however many things you ought to do, there are only so many things you can do at any one time. I was a busy woman . . . Killing Richard just wasn't a priority.

THE STRAY
BLACK DOG

> It is impossible to live with
> memory without falsifying it.

Chris Marker, Sunless

1. Black Dog

The worst thing about time is not having too little time, but too much. Time to swish around in, time to drown in. You are always remembering, or revising, or preparing, or rehearsing. Thinking, I ought to have told her then, right there in the café, that I loved her. What could have prevented me? . . . Thinking, When I see her next, I must be ready to show her that none of it touched me, that she didn't hurt me, that even her cruellest indifference couldn't injure me. Or I could apologise. I could quietly tell her, Catherine, after all this time, *even* after all this time, though so much has happened, I still love you. I could tell her that despite everything, despite the letters, despite the misunderstandings, despite the things that ought not to have been said or left unsaid, I still believe that she and I could be together. Or I could cause a scandal, barge into her classroom, hit her, or spit in her face, tell her that she is filth, that I detest her. The intruder in her classroom, the centre of an appalling scene, screaming, What right did you have? What gave you the right to think that you could annihilate me?

Yes, I can almost imagine myself doing that. You see, when you have too much time, time to drown in, you have time to be overwhelmed by the endless possibilities that finally become your consciousness of time. And you only know time as the consciousness of time.

I have certain dark feelings which are best described as an anxiety about the past. I have a persistent, probably unhealthy, concern that my crystal clear memory of events might falter, that my memory might not always summon the same images, or the same past, it summons now. I live in fear that fear will contaminate my memory.

A man who worked hard, who concerned himself with the wellbeing of others or the betterment of society, a decent man who lived selflessly and knew generosity of spirit, would never suffer in the way that a self-conscious man with too much time does.

Is having time on your hands so different to having blood on your hands?

If you wanted to punish a man who suffered from my temporal hyperconsciousness, you'd say something to make him doubt his memory, you'd question a small detail, or offer a new angle on an event, a reinterpretation subtle enough to make him fear that the composition of his memory is unstable, that things might be viewed differently, that he could have had everything wrong. If you wanted to punish such a man, you'd choose a word, or a phrase, or an image, that would explode like a stick of dynamite tossed into the still pool of memory. You could say to such a man, as Catherine said to me—Did she actually say this? Have I extrapolated from a misunderstood nuance?—Tim, I never loved you.

No, she couldn't have said that. I've had too much time to distort things, to rehearse and revise. So much time to hover above myself as a perpetual source of annoyance, like the

84

police helicopter in summer, a hyperconsciousness which has to keep prowling, questioning, and imagining in order to justify its own existence.

> You've been there before. You've seen it.
>
> Scotty to Madeleine, *Vertigo*

2. The Appropriation of Silence

Early in 1990, I enrolled as a student in a fiction writing course taken by the notable writer Bernard O'Connell. I was drawn to the course as much by my respect for O'Connell's books as his reputation as a teacher. O'Connell stood solidly behind classroom strategies that had served him well for more than a decade. We were to be instructed in the creation of literary fiction, and were expected to produce stories which might be suitable for publication in literary journals, such as *Approximate Life*, which then employed O'Connell as its fiction consultant.

In an act of good faith, Bernard O'Connell outlined his generic prejudices. He stated a strong personal distaste for fantasy, science fiction, and romance, and an impatience with stories that celebrated inner-suburban squalor—the sex and drug fests that had not yet been marketed as grunge. He also disliked hospital and funeral scenes. But his most particular aversion related to stories that were transparent works of revenge.

If students were to write stories that were, according to I.B. Singer's dictum, stories that only we could write, we were best advised to enter the world of our obsessions and preoccupations, to directly engage the emotional confusions we most fervently needed to understand. To avenge hurt by using one's imaginative power to turn the other into a monster—a one-dimensional embodiment of malicious intent—is too simple. The true artist would opt for the challenge of restoring the emotional world before the fall. The true writer would seek to investigate the original passion and attraction, to describe those things convincingly in a way that didn't betray the knowledge of what was to come. Memory is so susceptible to distortion and contamination, to defects of vision and revision. The challenge for the true artist is to pursue essential truths through the emotions, to seek truths that hurdle or permeate barriers constructed by the emotions.

Vindictiveness is cheap and ignoble, yet that lack of chivalry is part of its attraction. A vindictive writer becomes artful in the way that Satan's best agents become artful. You develop complex literary strategies to disguise base intent.

It was Catherine who had originally encouraged me to take Bernard O'Connell's writing course. She was more confident I would become a writer than I was at that time. But the commencement of my studies with Bernard O'Connell coincided with the termination of our friendship. I'd written a letter, sure that she would respond. I waited. I became desperate to speak to her, to clarify the situation, to gain some notion of how she understood my letter. Her only response was silence.

The year after Catherine's silence ended our friendship—the second year of my studies with Bernard O'Connell—I submitted a story called 'Packing Death', a version of which was later published in the scholarly journal *Approximate Life*.

I told myself that I wrote the story, a bizarre tale of a society under the sway of a mysterious death cult, as a form of exploration. The story was a means of trying to understand the long, self-destructive infatuation I had with Catherine. I was trying to find a way of dealing with everything that had been left so tenuously unresolved. I convinced myself that my story was not vindictive, but cathartic.

In my story, 'Packing Death', Catherine becomes Catherine O'Shaunessy. I might have chosen another name, but her name is common enough. And there is a certain charm in double-guessing. When is something so obvious that it is too obvious?

As I return to read 'Packing Death' now, five years after its original publication, I am struck by its technical inadequacies. That strange voice in the opening section, a voice which came to me in a dream, a voice intended to suggest a language spoken from beyond the death of meaning, for that's what the story was supposed to be about; the death of meaning, the death of essential communication, the death of good faith. Now I see it as a voice which draws too much attention to itself; 'this elegance notwithstanding . . . ', 'That said, she never enjoyed autopsying acquaintances.' It's too proud. The style is too precious by half.

Now I feel required to ask myself whether this story was ever a genuine therapeutic exercise, or just a highly coded retaliation, the author's vindictiveness hidden behind a self-effacement which is altogether too modest.

Catherine the historian becomes Catherine the forensic pathologist. When her surgical procedures fail to determine the cause of death, she is expected to inventively redefine the meaning of death. This Catherine is highly efficient at tearing people apart. I can't be certain exactly what I had in mind here. Perhaps this isn't intended as an attack on the historian Catherine so much as an attack on historians who devote insufficient attention to dominant assumptions about the nature of time, and the function of memory.

The dominant history just cannot rid itself of the presumption that Time is continuous and divisible, that one can take possession of the historical moment. Dates, and names, and place-names imply a certainty regarding location, integrity, and identity that can never rightfully be presumed. And memory is always the thing to be valued. Forgetting is always the deficit. Will it be left to a neurophysician like Oliver Sacks to write the first insightful, sympathetic History of Forgetting?

Catherine and I used to have long discussions about abstract concepts of time and memory. She has since edited a collection which claims to be about the relationship between memory and history. If we still spoke to each other, I would tell her that the book's insights never go far enough. The collection errs on the side of commonsense, and chronologicality, and the historian's dependence on a factual world that supposedly exists just beyond personal subjectivity. The scalpel never cuts beyond acceptable or palatable truths.

And Catherine the forensic pathologist becomes a hero of the people the way that Catherine the historian was a hero of mine. I idolised her. I extrapolated from the particular to the general in order to give due proportion to the emotional hold that Catherine had over me. I could never understand why everyone who became acquainted with her did not share my intense preoccupation with her.

At the time that I wrote 'Packing Death', I was a modestly successful writer of television comedy. It flatters my abilities to imagine that I, in any incarnation, could become a successful stand-up comic. But Richard's extreme morbidity and cowardice are my own. Was this strategy so transparent as it seems to me now? Richard's self-deprecation gives him licence no self-promoter could enjoy. He's the drowner who gets to flail at those who would rescue him from himself.

And so in the final section, 'Love is Colder than Death', I allow Catherine to take the reins. The illusion of magnanimity. The story becomes hers, and she must decide whether her treacherous lover should perish beneath the knife, or be spared to suffer the torture of her malicious indifference. My fictional character Catherine O'Shaunessy has been granted the modern woman's plea for an active, self-determining life, but she's been cooled to freezing point, dehumanised.

'What's that perfume you're wearing?' Richard asks at their first meeting. 'Formaldehyde!' And so I have created a silence for Catherine, inescapable as the silence Catherine condemned me to.

At this distance, I can't kid myself that the story is thera-peutic. Even if I never held the scalpel, I was fully conversant with the weaponry at my disposal. I knew that my story made a claim no practising historian could fail to recognise; I had expressed the power to appropriate. The writer as proprietor knows that he doesn't need to caricature or satirise someone in order to demean or injure them. By what right have I stolen Catherine's silence and made it my own?

She had encouraged me to take Bernard O'Connell's class. She encouraged me to believe that I could become a writer. Whether through accident, negligence, or design, Catherine hurt me, and 'Packing Death' was my retort. I cannot say whether she read the story when it was originally published, or how she might have understood the story had she done so.

O'Connell's written comments at the end of my first draft are typically intriguing. He avoids committing himself with regard to the literary quality of my prose, or its potential for publication, preferring a general comment that I would have found more oblique at the time than it seems now.

> *I read fiction in order to learn something that I could not*
> *learn by any other means. What I hope to learn from*
> *fiction is the property of the particular person:*
> *his view of the world (?)*
> *his private truth (?)*
> *the distillation of his personality (?)*
> *what only he knows (?)*

I knew that writing 'Packing Death' was my only hope of speaking directly to someone who did not wish me to speak to her. Was that improper, inappropriate? Who might claim proprietorship of the silence which exists between two friends who had never been able to speak private truths to each other?

> We are always one step removed from
> whatever historical moment we choose
> to construct, doomed to contaminate that
> moment with our phantoms, and betray
> its veracity and uniqueness with the
> falsifying limits of our sensory and
> emotional experience.
>
> Kohji Morimoto, *Approximate or Perish*

3. The Stray Black Dog

I was dining with Catherine. Ten years had passed since our first meeting, and another year would pass before the letter which silenced our friendship. It was a very pleasant sunlit interlude, a discussion no different to all our discussions in tone; lively and heartfelt. But some of the things that she said then, some of the ideas she planted in my mind, have gathered significance as time has passed.

We had been to see a French film, *Mystere Alexina*, and we were dining outdoors at a trattoria in Toorak Road. The late sun had turned Catherine's hair a gorgeous shade of honey-gold. We were both hunched over our plates. I was eating fettucini with an unusually hot matriciana sauce when Catherine said something that surprised me.

Catherine said that we'd both lived unusual lives, that many other people would envy the lives we'd led. This didn't surprise me as a remark about herself. Catherine *had* led an unusual life. She had lived in Baltimore, she had worked on a prawn trawler off the Queensland coast, she had smoked opium in Thailand, she had lived in an old green tram that she'd transported to a block of land in the countryside, she had studied in Rome, and she'd been chauffeur-driven in Egypt. She had earned a Ph.D., and her first book was soon to be published. She had a fabulous career ahead of her.

Catherine was in a relationship, but we seldom if ever spoke of our emotional or sexual lives.

My life had been nothing like Catherine's. Though I was twenty-nine years old, I still lived at home with my parents. I had worked a number of base-grade jobs in the state public service, only recently finding work in television. I'd had many nervous episodes. I had an M.A. in literary theory, I had seen thousands of films, I was impotent. I had known Catherine for more than ten years without once finding the courage to tell her that I loved her. Another person making the same remark about an unusual or enviable life might have been taking the piss, but not Catherine.

She must have imagined that the life which I led—introspective, uneventful, frightened—was as interesting as hers, an unusual life that a respectable person might envy. I desperately wanted to pursue her statement, to flush-out an underlying intent or message.

Could Catherine have imagined how often I had rehearsed kisses and seductions which never took place, how like an engineer on the Snowy River scheme I keenly desired to intervene on the course of her history? Could she have had any notion that the period between my head hitting the pillow and sleep belonged to her and her alone?

At home, later that night, I began to think about the things Catherine knew about me, the things she might remember as unusual, the things which might make my life seem attractive or admirable to an attractive person who had lived a very different life. While reflecting on these things, I found that something had altered. My memories were unstable, like a film that had been incorrectly mounted in the projector. More than that, it was as if an extra figure had entered the frame, so that the composition had changed, and the familiar perspectives were disturbed. A stray dog, sniffing and scratching at the edge of the frame, trying to bury something.

I tried to remember in detail episodes from my earliest meetings with Catherine, only to find that my memories had changed. They seemed overloaded. Her ambiguous, drunken farewell kiss in the doorway was fully papered-over with a regret which had never attended my recollection of the kiss previously.

If a girl, however drunk, kissed me fully on the lips, just thirty minutes after telling me, conspicuously in front of a group of friends, that she couldn't imagine me having a girlfriend . . . If a girl kissed me like that now, having just said what Catherine said to me . . . Well, I'd assume that she was waiting, that she wanted me to show her what I wanted, to show her that I wanted her. But how old was I then? Nineteen? I was scared. So I convinced myself that she was drunk, that she wouldn't have said those things, or kissed me in that way if she hadn't been drunk.

I find myself caught in the most excruciating swirl of events, the images warped and distorted as if stolen from *The Cabinet of Dr Caligari*. Even our very first meeting, a memory so often rehearsed, is not the same. I am in a crowded party of new undergraduates. A hot airless room full of smoke and cheap alcohol. The woman who introduces me to Catherine is not the woman I remember. And Catherine herself is neither so young nor so schoolgirlish. She is more knowing. She leans forward, both hands holding a white plastic cup full of wine. She is an eighteen-year-old girl with light blonde hair, and piercing eyes, an easy laugh, slightly rounded shoulders, as mine are also. When she leans forward to convey a vital intimacy about her life or a favourite author, it's as if she's carrying a weight, as if she's being pushed into the action by the part that she's been contracted to play in my future life. Nothing in this memory is as it really was; feckless, innocent. And perhaps I will never be able to recover that scene now. It's tainted by the fall. My memories are being seized by a force reaching into them; an editor, cutting, colourising,

92

distorting, construing, misconstruing, so that the story is no longer my own.

I was dining with Catherine. We had been to see a French film, *Mystere Alexina*. We were sitting at an outdoor table, and I was eating a plate of fettucini with a very hot matriciana sauce, when Catherine said something which surprised me.

She said, I'm sending a stray black dog into your memories, and little by little it's going to take everything back, because no matter how much you wanted me, however much you wanted me to want you, or wanted to believe that I wanted you, however much you remembered things, and wrote them down as you wanted to remember them, you can't make your memories mine. You can't possess me by setting yourself up as the curator of everything that once existed between us.

I was dining with Catherine. The sunlight was honey-gold through her hair. I was eating a plate of fettucini with matriciana sauce when Catherine did something that astonished me. She let a black dog off the leash.

She said, No matter what you think now, or thought then, or hoped then, I never loved you.

Did she really say that? Could she have said that, or am I imagining her words through the crushing frustration of her silence?

She never loved me.

AN EVENING WITH
WITH
BOO RADLEY

Irony's a real bitch sometimes. You meet a girl, and almost at the instant of first meeting, you make up your mind about her. You decide that she's attractive, or dull, or bossy, or insane, or worth sleeping with. And because you insist on doing this, you always make godawful mistakes, though it's seldom that you get to know how stupid these misjudgments were. But just once in a while, your imperceptiveness returns to club you over the head.

I read in this morning's paper that Shelley Thorsen won the Tony for Best Actress on Broadway. The report describes her one-woman show, *An Evening With Boo Radley*, as a *tour de force*. After rereading this report several times, there can be no doubt. This is the same Shelley Thorsen who once tried to abduct me in Montparnasse. Sweet, funny, fucked-in-the-head Shelley turns out to be the most famous woman I've met, and, if you discount two negligible Australian Prime Ministers, the most famous person full stop. Shelley has clout. The thing is—and this is the pointy end of the irony—when I met Shelley Thorsen in Paris, she was just a rich lunatic. She was a girl idiot enough to confuse me with a British film star.

* * *

If you've got to be alone in a big city, then Paris might be the best place to be, but I hadn't intended to be by myself in Paris that Christmas. The way I'd planned things, Paris was going to be my weapon of seduction.

I was crazy about a film publicist named Amber, but I kept on fucking-up just when she was at the point of surrendering to me. I'd botched things so often that only a big gesture could restore the balance. So I took out a loan and bought two air tickets to Paris, and booked a month's accommodation at the enticingly named Tim Hotel on the Rue d'Arivee. Paris was going to be cultural lubricant, an incitement to vital fluid exchange.

I'd planned to spring all this on Amber at a decisive moment. We'd be watching *Breathless* or *The Umbrellas of Cherbourg* on video at her place, I'd make a subtle reference to spending Christmas in the city of love, and we'd end the evening in a hot, slippery entanglement. (Amber is a voluptuous redhead, and I had been hanging out for some entangled slipperiness since our first meeting.)

I can't remember how advanced my preparations were. The quiet video evening at her place had been arranged, but I hadn't yet rented *The Umbrellas of Cherbourg*. (I'm not sure what it is, but one look at Catherine Deneuve's wallpaper sends women crazy with desire.) Maybe I'd begun to check use-by dates on my condoms. Then Amber called. I spoke rapidly like someone with a night of amorous exploration in mind. There was a longish pause. Amber told me that her mother had died.

Amber's family came from all over the place for the funeral. Given the suddenness—her mother was only just fifty—Amber seemed to cope pretty well. I told myself that a Christmas in Paris would be good for her, that I should just hold off telling her about the tickets and hotel for a couple of weeks.

As it happened, I never told Amber about the tickets. So far as she's concerned, there never was a month of romance, not even in prospect, or declined possibility. I hadn't seen her for a couple of days, and when I got back to my flat, there was a message on the answering machine. Amber had called from Pretoria. She'd made an impulsive decision to spend Christmas in South Africa with her brother, who was a diplomat there. She would stay on if she could find work.

Given the choice between spending the summer moping in Melbourne, or rugging-up to mope in Paris, I chose Paris.

* * *

Like I said earlier, if you have to be alone in a big city, Paris is the best place to be. Galleries and museums, fabulous bookshops and cemeteries. The patisseries are wonderful, the cheese is brilliant, and the wine is red. (With the refund from Amber's ticket, I found myself drinking better wine than I might have otherwise.) And there are the cinemas. Paris is a cinephile's heaven. You can guarantee that every film you've ever wanted to see will be showing somewhere in Paris.

So it was hardly the most miserable time of my life; walking, drinking, depleting the French stockpile of almond croissants, checking out the German Expressionists at the Tokyo Palace, and The Universe of Borges at The Bibliothèque Nationale. And every night after dinner, when it was too cold to walk, a couple of films. Sure, I would have liked to have had Amber snuggled on the other side of my expensive double bed, but the Cassavettes retrospective was a reasonable consolation for a man who gets off on film.

The only really bad time was Christmas Day itself. I walked. Stuffed myself full of pastries and cake. I wanted to eat a proper holiday feast, but I couldn't warm to the idea of eating by myself when so many Parisian families were out celebrating. In the evening, I knew that I was in need of comedy, and *Harold and Maude*, with its toe-tapping Cat Stevens soundtrack, has never failed me. Paris being Paris,

Harold and Maude was showing just around the corner from the Sorbonne.

And I did feel much better laughing at Bud Cort's multiple fake suicides, and Ruth Gordon's eccentric driving, sharing my laughter with a hundred people of different nationalities on a chilly Christmas night. It took my mind off Amber and the torrid sex that I might have been enjoying.

I was out the front of the cinema, wrapping a scarf around my neck in preparation for the stroll back to Tim Hotel when a tall, pretty girl approached me, camera in hand. Her voice soon gave her away as an American.

Would you mind taking my photograph? It would really mean a lot to me if you would take my photograph.

Sure. Not a problem.

And just my saying, Sure. Not a problem, sent this girl into paroxysms of delight.

Oh, I just love your voice. It's so charming.

Already I had a feeling that things were out of whack; the disproportionate enthusiasm, the premature assessment of my vocal charm. But this was a drop-dead gorgeous girl, slender with auburn hair, a fabulous smile, the whole package. And she spoke a near-approximation of English, unlike the multitudes of gorgeous girls who had been turning my head in the previous week. I certainly wasn't going to crush this enthusiasm to have me photograph her in front of one of Paris' least memorable cinemas. I might have imagined that she was an American college girl whose vacation project was to have her photograph taken in front of every cinema in Europe, and that would have been enough to make her exactly my sort of girl.

I asked her to pose so that the composition would be balanced by a string of Christmas lights in the street behind her, but she couldn't be bothered with my artfulness. She smiled a strange, automatic smile, I pressed the shutter button on the Polaroid, and my job was done. Then she ran to me, threw her arms around me, and kissed me.

Oh, you're so fabulous. I've loved everything that you've done. You've no idea what this means to me.

I had no idea what this meant to her.

Inviting me back to her apartment for a drink, she apologised for not having introduced herself.

You must excuse me, I'm at an advantage here, I know who you are, but I haven't told you my name. I'm Shelley. My apartment's a couple of blocks from here.

Of course, I had to go with her if only to find out just who the fuck Shelley thought I was. I do have chameleonic features. I've been taken for a local in Scotland, Germany, France, and Italy. I can look Jewish. But this was more specific. She had someone in mind, and I was intrigued. I can't pretend that sex wasn't a part of it. She was a fabulous looking girl, and I was open to the idea of trading fluids with her. But I'm not an opportunist or a shit when it comes to sex. I'm quite fussy really. I don't have to believe that I'm in love with the girl, but I like to feel that nothing I know of would *preclude* my falling in love with her. That's why I didn't tell Shelley straight out, Hey, I think you're confusing me for someone. I knew that I wouldn't want to go back to her place if the misapprehension was outrageous.

With hindsight, I can say that I would have been extremely worried had I known that Shelley thought I was the actor Hugh Grant.

I expected that Shelley's apartment would be the typical one-bedroom dive in the middle of the student quarter. Not so. A full-time security guard received her in the foyer. An antique lift took us up to the fourth floor. Shelley's apartment was tastefully lavish. Very modern. Her kitchen adjoined a massive living room. Beautifully framed Chagall and Miro prints on the walls. A television set slightly larger than Dr Who's Tardis. The whole deal must have cost a fortune.

Well, I said, this is fantastic. I had you marked down as a student.

Did you? Did you really? . . . Well, no. I'm not a student. But this isn't mine. It belongs to my parents. They work in Chicago mostly, so they let me have this place while I'm rehearsing.

Rehearsing?

Oh, you don't want to know about that, she said, handing me a glass of red wine.

I must have said something like, Mmm, yes, y-yes, tell me about it, because whatever I mumbled made her go off like a pornographic actress in the final reel.

Say that again! *Please!* Say it just like you said it then.

Tell me about it.

No, *with the stuttering*. It's that thing you do in *Bitter Moon*. I saw *Bitter Moon* four times. I'm your biggest fan.

I think you're mistaking me for someone else, I . . .

There's no need to be shy. I'm not going to kidnap you or anything. I'm not a whacko, if that's what you're worried about.

Up until that point, the thought of abduction hadn't crossed my mind.

That's such a weird fucking film, *Bitter Moon*. Really weird. Polanski's a strange man . . . Did he ever speak to you about Charles Manson and that stuff?

Shelley thumped the pillows next to where she was sitting on the sofa. Come and sit here. I've got so many things to ask you about.

I'd seen *Bitter Moon* not long before. I hated it. Peter Coyote's close to Julian Sands and Richard Dreyfus on my list of Box Office Poison. I could picture the mannered, wimpish, affectedly indecisive Home Counties actor that Shelley was confusing me for, but I couldn't remember his name. (All this was well before *Four Weddings and a Funeral*, and the blow-job in the back of the car.) I knew that he and I looked nothing alike. He had an Oxbridge accent, and mine was conspicuously Melbourne-nasal. The only thing that we might have had in common was an inability to look attractive women in the eye when speaking to them.

No, Polanski's never actually said anything about Charles Manson to me, I told Shelley. I don't think it's something he likes to dwell on.

Her hand was rubbing my thigh, and my thigh was enjoying it more than my head felt that it should.

You're going to be *so* famous. I can tell. I have a fantastic ability for predicting the future.

I could predict that Shelley's hand would be inside my Levis at any moment. I thought that I should change the subject on behalf of the actor she was confusing me for, so that he didn't get a reputation for being easy.

But you must tell me about your own work. What are you rehearsing?

Do you really want to know?

Sure.

This succeeded in removing Shelley's hand from my person. It seemed that she wouldn't be able to talk about her work while groping me.

It's a one-woman show. It's going to be epic. Very expensive. It goes for five-and-a-half hours without an interval.

If I hadn't been determined to stay in character, I might have exclaimed, Five-and-a-half hours without an interval! You're fucking kidding! I opted for a polite, That must be exhausting.

Have you seen the movie version of *To Kill a Mockingbird*?

Sure. Gregory Peck. Robert Duvall. It's a classic.

That's what I'm doing.

You're doing a one-woman stage version of *To Kill a Mockingbird*?

No. Not a stage version. I'm doing the film. I'm telling the

103

film . . . Just me. No props. No costumes. Not any music. I'm recreating the emotional experience of the film.

I had a premonition then. And it wasn't about my fame as a British actor in Hollywood, or getting sucked-off on the back seat of a car. I took a discreet look at my watch. It was 12.45. My premonition had to do with a five-and-a-half hour show without intervals. A show that had a PATRONS MUST PISS AND SHIT BEFORE ENTRY sign on the door. This was the show that was about to unfold before my eyes.

And I should head-off your informed curiosity, because it's exactly the question that was going through my mind, How can a film which runs no longer than two hours become a five-and-a-half hour performance?

Well, it wasn't a this-then-this and then-that account of the plot an excited twelve-year-old might relate. Shelley did everything, *became* everything. Not only did she do the voices and describe the actions and interactions, she did the music and sound effects and described the crosscutting and the camera movements and shot-sizes, while offering an elegant, ironic commentary on what the characters might have thought they were doing, or would have preferred to be doing.

In *The Purple Rose of Cairo*, a character comes down off the screen to enter Mia Farrow's life, but Shelley dragged you up through her imaginary screen so that you could smell Walter Cunningham's syrup as he poured a half-jug over his meat and greens. You felt the panic as Jem's trousers caught on the barbed wire. I became oblivious to Shelley's performance. That was the brilliance of the thing. I never sat back and said, By Christ, that's the best Gregory Peck I've ever seen, how could a young woman capture the resonance of Gregory Peck's voice so perfectly?, because I was so seized by the immediacy of events, too much a part of things to stand back. And I can't tell you how good her Gregory Peck was. But everyone was equally good. You felt the heat of the courtroom, and trembled before Ewell's evil bigotry, though Shelley's *pièce de résistance* was the Mad Dog scene.

One moment Shelley is the mad dog hopping and bopping at the end of the street, the next she's the maid Calpurnia herding Scout and Jem through the front door. Cal calls Atticus, and Atticus drives over with his colleague, Hec. Of course, no-one expects Atticus to do anything practical, he's a lawyer, a man of learning, but Hec passes Atticus the rifle. Atticus twitches around getting a sight of the target. Shelley the mad dog is still rolling and lurching towards him. Atticus throws away his glasses.

Bang!

The dog drops dead. Perfect fucking shot. The Finch kids are totally disbelieving, mouths wide open. Shelley's Atticus tries awfully hard not to be smug about this.

'Don't go near that dog, d'ya understand? He's just as dangerous dead as alive.'

But it's Shelley's Hec who offers Jem and Scout a picture of the world before their world began. He tells them what they never knew, that their daddy was the best shot this side of the Mississippi.

Well, the mad dog sure the fuck knows that. Dead and foamy-mouthed on the gravel. Any attempt to translate all this for you, to communicate to you the kaleidoscopic brilliance of Shelley's world, is bound to fail. It should never be permissible for a writer to tell you that you had to be there, but you had to be there. I heard the shots, the violins, I was spat on and snatched away by evil men, I sweated and trembled. Shelley was electrifying.

When it came to those final scenes, when Scout is finally introduced to poor Boo Radley, Boo the hero who has just saved her brother's life, I was positively blubbering away in front of Shelley the enchantress. Poor Boo playing possum behind the bedroom door.

'Hey, Boo.'

Atticus always the well-mannered host.

'Miss Jean-Louise, Mr *Arthur* Radley . . . I believe he already knows you.'

The sweep of soppifying violins. The final voice-over above the montage of the wide streets and images of Atticus' perfect fatherdom, all full of the loss of the Eden we once had, and the knowledge of serpents and redeemers. Closing titles.

Shelley was standing in front of me, entirely spent. I was sitting in front of her, every emotion drained from me. Inconceivable as it might have seemed just at that moment, I was in Shelley's apartment in Paris. The old south had vanished. Five-and-a-half hours had passed.

Shelley, that was . . . That was . . .

No, it wasn't. I don't think that I had Tom and Mayella. Mayella's generally my best turn, but I just couldn't get her tonight. Mayella's like that . . . Would you like a drink or something, Hugh? Maybe we should just go to bed. The sun will be up soon.

A drink would be great.

I'm thinking, Hugh? Hugh? *Hugh Grant!* That's right. She thinks that I'm Hugh Grant. Somewhere amid all the Scout-this, and Yer a nigger-lover, Mr Finch-thats, I managed to forget that a relatively unknown British actor had inspired this whole astonishing performance.

And this same Hugh Grant was now expected to give a performance of his own. If I'd given in to the call of my trousers, I'd have fucked Shelley right then underneath her plastic Christmas tree, she was beautiful beyond belief, but there was an Atticus Finch inside my head offering sage advice. Richard, when I was a boy, my daddy told me something that I've never forgotten. He said, Son, you can sleep with all the cheerleaders you like, you can have a threesome with your teacher and the blackboard monitor, but son, it's a sin, *a sin before God*, to sleep with someone who thinks that you're Hugh Grant.

I had time to think these things because after making me a stiff gin and tonic, Shelley disappeared into another room. I just knew that she'd come back in a transparent negligée, and all Atticus' best advice would go right out the window. Trying to convince myself, you can't fuck this girl. It would be dead wrong. She might be a genius, she might have just given the most devastating theatrical performance since Booth shot Lincoln, but she's so nutty she couldn't walk down the street without being jumped on by squirrels.

I did my best to imagine Amber in South Africa. I tried to persuade myself that I owed Amber fidelity. However fierce or earnest the internal debate, if my host had returned in anything even vaguely skimpy or transparent, the Don't Jump on Shelley lobby would have been vanquished.

Ten, maybe fifteen minutes passed. When Shelley returned, she was clothed as she had been when she departed, but she was carrying a very large photo album, the type with tissue-paper dividers. She was still very excited.

I'm so thrilled that you liked my show. And I'm even more thrilled that I can put your photograph in my album.

I hadn't really looked at the Polaroid when it developed, and I wasn't that keen to examine it now. Shelley, for all her strangeness, was a remarkably handsome young woman, and my snapshot didn't flatter her in the slightest. I was shocked to discover that her album was full of similar, hastily snapped photographs. All had Shelley as their subject.

They all seem to be photographs of you.

Yes, but yours is very special to me, Hugh. I'm going to give it a page all by itself.

You really should let photographers take more time. None of these shots do you justice.

Oh! No, of course not. They're not meant to. That's not the point. It's a kind of private joke. It wouldn't matter if I wasn't in them, but me being the subject unifies the whole deal.

And what is the deal?

107

She turned the pages to show me the first photograph. It was taken in the street at night. Shelley looks nervous. Her smile is forced. She's overlit. Too close to the flash.

Do you know who took that photograph, Hugh?

I wasn't game to speculate. I had no idea how Hugh Grant would answer such a question.

Woody Allen.

Bullshit!

That's what everyone says, but it's true! A couple of years back, I was in a small side street near the Pompidou Centre. I'd just finished photographing something. And this man came around the corner towards me. It was Woody Allen. Well, I lifted up my camera, a reflex thing, my one chance to take Woody Allen's photograph, and the poor man . . . He was like a vampire confronted with a crucifix. He had his arm up over his eyes, saying, No. No. *Please*.

Well, I apologised. I didn't know what had come over me. I don't ordinarily intrude on people like that. And Woody was gracious and nice about it. So I asked him a favour, whether he'd take *my* photograph, so that I'd know I had a photograph taken by Woody Allen. And Woody joked about whether he could be trusted not to steal my camera, but there it is. A Portrait of the Artist as a Young Woman by Woody Allen.

That's amazing! But what are all these? I asked. She had maybe eighty or ninety of these snaps in her album.

That's the weirdest thing. After that night, it got like my camera was a magnet for famous people. I only needed to go out for a walk at night, and, *voilá*!

She began to point at the snaps.

Boris Becker took that . . . And that was Beatrice Dalle. I was worried about asking her because she looks so fierce and unpredictable, but she thought it was hilarious. Most of these people, they think that it's the funniest thing. They're all so relieved that I'm not trying to photograph them . . . That was Charles Aznavour, and that was Milan Kundera. That was

Mick Jagger, that was Barbara Walters, and that one there was Naomi Wolf . . . Let me see that one . . . That was Liv Ullmann, I think . . . Where's my favourite?

She turned over several pages.

There!

It was a picture of Shelley in the street at night, just as all the others were pictures of Shelley in the street at night.

Who do you think took that?

Margaret Thatcher?

You're close! . . . No, *Mikhail Gorbachev*! He was *so* nice. He wanted me to take a photograph of him, or to have another man take a photograph of me with him, but I refused. I have this sense of purity. If I started letting people who aren't famous take my photograph, the camera would cease to be enchanted.

My heart sank then. By allowing myself to be mistaken for Hugh Grant, I'd put the enchantment of Shelley's Polaroid at risk.

But it only took a moment for a more cynical thought to cross my mind.

Shelley, you'd be surprised how few people ask me to take their photograph. Not that many people recognise me, especially here in Paris.

Now maybe. But I just know that you're going to be more famous than William Hurt . . . Y'know, only three people have ever refused me: Francois Mitterand, William Hurt, and Sandrine Bonnaire.

Being a cinema buff, I knew who Sandrine Bonnaire was, but not many would.

Well, maybe it wasn't Sandrine Bonnaire. Are you sure that you couldn't have been confusing her with someone else?

If I'd abducted Shelley's mother, and begun to roast her over an open fire, I couldn't have provoked a more outraged reaction.

Just what the fuck's that meant to mean?

Only, well, you know, that you might see someone and think that it's William Hurt, or . . . Sandrine Bonnaire, and they might just be someone who looks a bit like them. Especially in the dark.

Hey! . . . *Fuck you!* If you're going to call me a liar, call me a liar straight to my face. Tell me this photograph wasn't taken by Woody Allen, that it could have been taken by any fucking idiot in the street. That this snap wasn't taken by Sting, that it was just some 45-year-old English millionaire who looked and sounded and smelled like Sting . . .

Shelley ripped the Sting photograph out of the album, and hurled it across the room.

You might be a charming fucking actor, Hugh, I know that you're going to be famous, but you can't call me a liar. You've got no fucking right to do that. I'm going to be more famous than you. One day, someone just like me will ask me to take their photograph.

I could hardly argue with the logic of that.

Look, I'm sorry Shelley. It's very late. You're tired after doing the show for me. I think that I should go back to my hotel now.

I can't believe this! You're *dumping* me. I do my show for you, I make you drinks, I show you my photographs, and now you call me a liar, and dump me, just like that. Well, I don't need your fucking photograph, Hugh. I'm the only fucking American in Paris who knows who you are, and now I don't give a shit.

Shelley ripped the photograph that I'd taken. It seemed to me that she was doing something profane, something that I regretted. Maybe I regretted it more than she would later.

You don't mean that, I said, putting my hands on her shoulders to calm her down. You're just tired. You misunderstood me, Shelley. I didn't mean that at all. Of course you wouldn't have confused someone who wasn't William Hurt with William Hurt. That's not what I meant.

You're right, I am tired. Stay with me, Hugh. Make love to me.

Skimpy negligées work much better than psychotic episodes when it comes to persuading me to act against my better judgment.

No, I have to go. We'll see each other again. I promise.

When? . . . You're just saying that.

No. No, not at all . . . Tonight. Um, yeah, I'll meet you outside the entrance to Luxembourg Metro. Seven. No, eight. Eight outside Luxembourg.

Tonight at eight.

Shelley kissed me tenderly on the lips, but I couldn't wait to hear her door shut behind me, to get down the stairs, and out into the real world. If I could have eradicated sexual desire at that moment, I might have been tempted to. I felt like a true enemy of the people.

And Shelley looked so ineffably lovely, standing there in her doorway. All shagged-out, insane longing.

Tonight. Don't be late. . . . And Hugh, *je t'aime*.

It was nearly nine. Outside, Parisians were bustling past in the sleeting rain. An old man walking toward me hit the edge of a dog turd with his heel, and skidded three metres, but kept his balance heroically. I might have liked to grab him by the collar. I might have liked to interrogate him. Do you think that I look the slightest fucking bit like Hugh Grant? I refrained. The old turd-surfer had better things to do. And so did I. I slept like a baby.

Maybe this story should end with a warm southern voice-over, with a woman who sounds just like the narrator of *To Kill a Mockingbird* saying something to restore gentleness to my tale. You must have guessed that I had no intention of waiting for Shelley outside the Metro entrance. I felt bad about it, but she was waiting for someone famous, or someone who was on the verge of becoming famous, which is exactly what Hugh Grant did, probably thanks to Shelley's voodoo Polaroid.

I wandered around Paris by myself for another week, avoiding the cinema, desperately hoping that I wouldn't run into Shelley, but still fantasising about the fabulous sex that we might have had if she hadn't compelled me to make an adverse judgment about her sanity. I told myself that I would have been taking advantage of her, that it was morally indefensible. For me to have slept with a poor touched soul who thought that I was a British actor . . . well, a decent, heroic man like Atticus Finch wouldn't do that. It would've been like fucking a mockingbird.

At the precise time that Shelley would have been waiting outside Luxembourg Metro, I was sitting in a café writing a letter to Amber in South Africa. I told Amber that I wanted to marry her. I was going to write plays. They would be famous plays, I was sure of it. All I needed was her love, and an ounce of good fortune, a lucky break.

I didn't marry Amber. I never even heard from her again. She shacked up with a journalist in Kenya. I have written plays, but no-one will produce them. I have no connections, no famous theatrical figure to champion them. Shelley might have.

Could Shelley have loved me if I wasn't British? Could she have looked me in the eyes and said, Richard, *je t'aime*? She has her Tony now. She's as famous as anyone needs to be. No-one who wanted to be anyone would refuse an invitation to sleep with her. Everyone will want to take her photograph.

FOREVER

In his fondest memories, she will be in jeans and barefooted, kicking foam at the water's edge, playful in the heat and the white light, dizzy with her own laughter, pressed tight against the blue sky, and tight to his lips.

She will remember him most for the words that didn't come, how strangely ill at ease he was with emotion, so beautifully childish, and how she wanted to help him speak the words of affection that seemed laden with every fear he had ever known.

She will always remember their time in Zurich, his excitement at seeing Einstein's laboratory, and the way that he spoke about Einstein with so much more tenderness than he spoke about his own father.

He will distinctly remember the sensation of pushing inside her the first time, though he will also remember wishing that she was Catherine, knowing that her initial attraction for him had been her physical likeness to Catherine.

Not once will he ever feel tempted to call her, to apologise, or to beg forgiveness. He will feel neither remorse nor a curiosity to discover her remaining feelings for him.

She will never understand why the sight of the colour green, or the mention of the colour green, brings his face to mind, how the two things, his face and the colour green, came to be associated in her memory.

In the months following their split, he will begin to question whether he ever loved her.

In those first weeks after the separation, she will fantasise about breaking into his house and erasing all his computer files. She will delight in the thought of destroying his back-up disks and hard copies, feeling that the destruction of six years research would balance the pain in her heart.

Inevitably, she will come to believe that his dissatisfaction was her fault.

When he explains the bust-up to his male friends, he will tell them that their problem had been sex, her lack of interest, and as the years pass, he will gradually convince himself of the truth of this explanation.

He will never again wear the black shirt that she liked so much.

Years later, she will try to persuade herself that she has forgotten him, that he no longer has the power to damage her ego, but his name will bubble to the surface in her conversation. She will stumble across his name when she means to speak of someone else. His name will power upward into her consciousness like an eruption.

Sometimes, rereading avowals of love for him in her diary, she will feel debased, as if History had taken a black texta and drawn the Fuhrer's moustache on her upper lip.

To soothe a new wife, he will manufacture a jaundiced version of the eighteen months that he spent with her, referring to it as 'my temporary insanity'.

She will always remember him on his birthday.

He will never remember her birthday.

Yet when he encounters handwriting on a letter that resembles her handwriting, he will be disconcerted by a sudden breathlessness and quickening of the pulse.

Though hers will be the more truthful memory, he will recall many of the things that she would choose to forget, like the horrified expression on her face when he referred, for the first and only time, to her cunt.

She will always stew over what he meant when he described her as an emotional terrorist, and she will never arrive at a definitive answer.

After the split, they will meet again just nine times in the forty-one years before his death. Neither of them will ever appreciate that these forty-one years define the limit of what they once referred to as forever.

CRIMINAL HISTORY

1. Protection

Life is full of character-building experiences, and near the top of my list of such experiences is Acting Senior Sergeant Ross Headlam. It's hard to say what sort of person Ross started out as, but police work hadn't been kind to him. Most days, he gave the impression that he'd woken up chin-deep in a bath full of snot and expected his fortunes to slide.

I don't dislike coppers. I worked with plenty of them. A copper can seem like a reasonable person when you're talking about football or grog, or when they're describing their past acts of heroism, but only a fool would engage a copper in discussion about the future of society. No-one confused Ross Headlam with a reasonable human being, and no-one ever sought his views on the future of society. You didn't need to.

My desk was two metres away from the desk where Ross spent the first two hours of each shift reading the newspaper and muttering to himself. Over a period of weeks, I began to recognise this meditation as his process of extrapolating the general from the particular. Ross never passed comments or observations about individual news stories, or photographs, or comic strips, he'd just gather it all up and toss it into the pot his psyche was stewing. Finally, sentences began to form.

You can't tell me that this computerisation is a step forward.

Or, You know what smog is, Timmy?

You knew that you weren't expected to answer this question. Your duty was to be silent while Ross told you what smog is.

It's got nuthin' to do with exhaust fumes or that crap at all. Smog is the product of human negativity.

Usually after such an utterance, Ross closed his newspaper and disappeared to the toilet for an hour. His concentration was intense.

One morning, I saw Ross gaze at that day's horoscope page for seventy-five minutes. His phone rang twice but he didn't answer.

You know what the future is, Timmy? . . . The future is the sum of all possible threats. The future is a dark storm of heinousness waiting to break.

After a meeting with the Commissioner and his senior advisers, Acting Senior Sergeant Ross Headlam returned to the office, and approached my desk carrying a dozen bottles of liquid paper and a mission statement.

Timmy, my boy, you have acquired new duties.

And what might they be, Ross?

Your new job is to protect the officers who protect us from themselves. These might look like bottles of whiteout, but they're the clerical version of the morning-after pill. They offer post-hoc contraception to history's innocents.

2. The Bat Phone

Back in 1987, with economic rationalism still in its infancy, the world was full of undemanding clerical jobs in large government offices, sheltered workshops where the confused could stop and catch their breath on the way to wherever they were meant to be going. As a failed teacher who dreamt of becoming a writer, I spent twelve months working as a clerk in the Information Bureau of the Victorian Police Department.

A large staff of shift-working public servants did the dog-work for the uniformed police who ran the office. Mostly, the clerks answered telephone and telex enquiries, and supplied criminal records information to officers in police cars, stations, or the major squads. There were several positions of slightly greater responsibility. One of them involved the administration of the Bat Phone.

Only the authorised Bat Phone operator was permitted to give out information requested via the Bat Phone. These information requests came from agencies entitled to receive confidential criminal records information: bodies such as the Federal Police, Prison Release, Customs, or the National Crime Authority. Any breakdown in strict procedure, a failure to check an authority code, might result in highly sensitive information falling into the hands of felons, or corrupt officials.

I've always shunned responsibility, and I had no ambition to take on the Bat Phone. The microscopic increase in pay was no incentive. Given the choice, I would have preferred to engage in basic duties that required very little thought, automatic tasks which left space for fruitful daydreaming. I was not given the choice.

When Dale, the evening shift Bat Phone operator, was forced to take extended sick leave, Ross Headlam deemed that I was the only person sufficiently discreet and trustworthy to replace him. I might have been flattered by the judgment if I hadn't perceived a certain irony.

Discretion had never been my predecessor's forte. The extravagantly catty Dale was a dedicated member of the Collingwood Cheer Squad. He spent most of his time assessing and discussing the physical attributes of Collingwood footballers, most particularly the tightness of their shorts, and the linimented sheen of their robust thighs. Dale frequently boasted that he'd slept with two of these gods, an indiscretion which might not have threatened his wellbeing if he hadn't been foolish enough to name the footballers concerned in front of police and public servants who moved in football circles. Dale's workmates were told only that he would take nine months to recover from an unfortunate accident.

Answering the Bat Phone was not the only duty assigned to the Bat Phone operator. During quiet times, you were expected to crosscheck work returned from the typists, and to organise searches for missing files. None of this threatened to compromise my personal values. However, my second month in the job coincided with the issue of a directive by the most senior police officials. Ross Headlam returned from a meeting carrying a dozen bottles of liquid paper, and placed them on my desk.

I had a new duty. My task was to protect serving officers from their worst literary instincts.

So began my brief career as a Stalinist reviser of criminal history.

3. Additional Particulars

Midway through the 1980s, the Victorian government began to extend the provisions of the Freedom of Information Act. As these extensions became more pervasive, senior police became nervous about the possibility of public access to documents held at the Information Bureau.

One grey area of the new legislation, so far as it related to the endless mounds of documents held at the Information Bureau, involved gratuitous police judgments and predictions concerning the character, behaviour, and future criminality of recorded criminals.

Victorian police were as unfond of paperwork as they were

of criminals. Members of the force were inclined to write unflattering and indelicate opinions of convicted offenders in the 'Additional Particulars' section of the Antecedent Form, otherwise known as a Two-Ten. The senior executives of the department were concerned that any public access to these forms would leave the department and individual officers open to writs connected to libels, and defamations, or to charges of sexual and racial discrimination. And officers didn't always stop at offering their opinions about the criminal subject of their report. They often passed adverse comment about family members, relationships, nationalities, organisations, living conditions, and lifestyles.

My task was to save as much information as might prove valuable, but to whiteout any remarks which might conceivably cost the department (and, by implication, the Victorian taxpayer) big money.

To describe an offender as 'vile and disgusting' might have been within the bounds of legal acceptability, but not so his innocent de facto wife, and as this information was hardly crucial in either instance, both remarks could be whited-out. 'Her record suggests that she is an inveterate offender' could remain, likewise, 'Her record suggests that she is likely to commit further offences', and 'Her record suggests that she will continue to come under police attention'. But 'Her long record indicates that she will continue to offend' was too risky and required obliteration.

These speculations on the probability of future offence presented the greatest threat to the financial wellbeing of the author. It was not in an officer's interests to be publicly exposed as the author of a prediction like 'this filth will continue to predate', no matter how soundly based according to principles of inductive reasoning. So you slathered on the whiteout.

But at another level, I began to become fascinated with the police officers' implied view of time, history, and human evolution. You could hardly fail to recognise that their casual speculations about human nature and the possibility of ordered society would make a fruitful area of study for criminologists or psychologists in as much as these unguarded observations began to suggest a collective police psyche. In my experience with the liquid paper bottle, the essential characteristics of this psyche were: a jaundiced or deterministic view of human nature, intense cynicism and pessimism, and a tendency for racial and class stereotyping.

Strike 'human vermin'.

Strike 'typically hopeless abo'.

Strike 'noxious little pillow biter'.

According to this generalised psyche, anyone who had been convicted of an offence, or anyone who had been *caught* offending once, was, almost without fail, someone who had long been engaged in undetected felonious activity. His or her status as a 'criminal' would, by definition, demonstrate an inclination to the pursuit of crime.

These predictions indicated a police force which envisaged an entropical future where perceived inevitabilities governed the breakdown of societal order. Offenders and offences would breed and multiply. When called upon to speculate about the future in the form of the collected individuals who would shape and inform it, the average police officer imagined a less than brave new world.

I slathered on the whiteout, conscious that I was doing a snow job on a version of the future. But I couldn't be sure whether my liberal applications of liquid paper were removing or manufacturing the preconditions for zero visibility.

I did know that the worst thing that could happen to me, both as a clerk, and a prospective citizen of the third millennium, was to imagine myself into the future that police imagined; a world of predetermined violation and indecency, a world of escalating chaos and genetically programmed malfeasance.

4. A Society Based On Competition

Ross Headlam only became animated when he collected money. Apart from reading the paper, crapping, and offering haiku on concepts in need of redefinition, his most important duty was to organise raffles, the football-tipping competition, the Tattslotto syndicates, and any other competition which took his fancy. When Ross approached with a folder in his hand, you knew the speediest way to get rid of him was to reach into your pocket and cough up the required cash.

How much am I up for this time?

Two bucks.

What's the prize?

Two hundred.

Shit!

The rest goes towards the Christmas Party.

And what do I have to do?

You've got to guess the Christian name of the first criminal—charged, not cautioned—born in the 1980s.

Jesus, Ross! That'd make him seven now. Half the staff here will leave before you have to pay out.

No way, Timmy. We'll have one in the next month or two. A little thief, or an arsonist. You mark my words.

Yeah, well, O.K . . . I'll take Jason.

Already taken.

Shane.

Nah, mate. Shane's gone.

Brad or Brett? . . . I'll go for Brett.

Brett it is. Good luck.

That was the last I expected to hear of Ross' Criminal Prodigy competition during my time in the office. Yet true to Ross' intuition, just three weeks later a winner was announced.

As it happened, the hot favourites Jason and Shane were rolled by a Mark, born in April, 1980. Bernie Peperkamp pocketed the two hundred dollars.

127

Hey, Ross. This kid, Mark, what's he up for?

Guess.

Shop-lifting?

Worse than that.

Substance abuse and car theft?

Worse than that.

Worse than drugs and car theft! He's seven, fer Chrissake!

Rape, and aggravated sexual assault.

Nah, you're kidding me.

Little brat held a screwdriver to a kid's neck while his ten-year-old brother fucked him up the arse.

No way! You're fucking kidding.

That's the future, Timmy. It's coming soon to a suburb near you.

5. Criminal Science

We're all capable of living down to our lowest opinion of ourselves. I think that criminals are better off not being able to read their own police files. And not just because many of the things said about them, their families, and friends are highly speculative and ill-informed. If it was possible for a criminal to read his or her own file as a disinterested observer might read it, they would probably decide that they didn't amount to much. They would see themselves as expendable citizenry.

I happen to subscribe to the view of an essential human nature. We don't really change much from what we start out as. Certain conditions will invariably, perhaps automatically, activate predisposed drives. Which isn't to say that I'm sold on the science of predicting criminal behaviour. Who can say which of those many essential drives were most essential till after they've been brought into effect? For a science to right-fully call itself a science, it must have a strong predictive capacity. Criminologists have always displayed their greatest expertise when invited to be wise after the event.

Immediately after the Second World War, the British penal system bought heavily into the notion of criminology as a predictive science. Juvenile offenders, even those who had committed relatively petty crimes, were subjected to exhaustive psychological profiling in the belief that intense scrutiny might lead to an accurate forecast of future outcomes. But there is a difficulty with this. Even the criminally disposed have a myriad of criminal potentials.

As a fourteen-year-old in Borstal, Ronald Biggs confessed to an expert in adolescent psychiatry that he often masturbated. This admission led the expert to predict that young Ronnie would likely come to police attention as a sex offender. And maybe if Biggs had been less successful as a bank robber, his thoughts would have turned to a second avenue of criminality. But the so-called scientific approach to antisocial behaviours would seem to tell us less about potential sex-offenders and train robbers than it does about a once-prevalent social distaste for masturbation.

Cardinal Newman's famous credo about the child at seven being a blueprint of the adult to come probably holds, but how do we estimate which of many different traits will come to the fore, or become dominant?

At age seven, my ambition was to become a television scriptwriter. I dreamed of writing episodes of my favourite show, *The Man From UNCLE*, a very popular American spy spoof which then screened on Channel 7 at eight-thirty on Thursday nights. That was the sacred hour of the week for me.

The Man From UNCLE was pretty much dead and buried by the time I was ten, but by age twenty-eight I found myself writing sketch comedy for a highly successful television show (the title, *Fast Forward*, is itself ironic in this context) which went to air on Channel 7 at eight-thirty on Thursday nights.

Was any of this inevitable? It certainly wouldn't have seemed so inevitable fifteen months earlier when I was still slopping whiteout on indiscreet speculations and predictions.

Had I known that my future was predestined, that I was genetically programmed to write television scripts which went to air on Channel 7 at eight-thirty on Thursday nights, I might have saved myself years of unnecessary distress and worry. One of the times when I was most worried about where life might be heading was sitting at a desk opposite Acting Senior Sergeant Ross Headlam, shaking my liquid paper bottles so that their precious contents wouldn't go dry and crusty.

6. History As A Piece of Work

After reviewing so many documents in so many files, you began to get an appreciation of the police officer as historian. They were authors of a hidden history, fashioning a subcultural version of the culture for a privileged readership of (presumed) shared values.

With so many contributors to this history over such a prolonged stretch of time, I was surprised that my attention could be drawn to the style of individual authors. Certain themes and motifs would recur with sufficient frequency to convey a picture of a distant police officer. One historian who comes to mind is Senior Constable Davis.

In the Additional Particulars section of four Two-Tens relating to four separate (male) offenders, Senior Constable Davis opined that the offender would be unlikely to completely reject the criminal way of life unless he 'distanced himself from the piece of work sharing his bedroom'.

I took 'piece of work sharing his bedroom' to come within the terms of my guidelines for erasure, and applied the liquid paper in all four instances, but not without a thought for

Senior Constable Davis. I imagined him pulling a frozen dinner out of his freezer as he contemplated all the pieces of work who would bring a man undone in this city, thankful that he had been able to distance himself from the piece of work who so nearly warped his soul.

7. The Sunrise Clause

Not once in my experience did a police officer completing the Additional Particulars section of the Two-Ten offer the opinion that the offender would certainly not offend again, that in spite of his past crimes he would choose to marry a nice girl and live in a pretty white house with his wife, three children and a cocker spaniel, that he might decide to write perceptive books which offered useful insights into his own past, and criminality *per se*; that his future life, and the lives of many others he would meet, had probably been informed and enriched by his brush with infraction.

8. A Crime of Convenience

However much I might have wanted to protect those who protect us from themselves, I hadn't been a police officer, and I would never be entirely privy to the mysteries of the law enforcer's psyche. Once I made the mistake of asking Ross to speculate on those who committed Melbourne's notorious, unsolved, Great Bookie Robbery.

We'll never know who did that. They might as well close the file.

But what if the same gang struck again and left new clues?

If that mob strikes again, they won't leave any clues. Those blokes are criminal masterminds.

They're *what*! . . . You mean they got lucky. They silenced the right witnesses, had everything fall into place. They struck a bunch of detectives who didn't ask the right people the right questions, or might not have *wanted* to ask the right questions.

Luck had nothing to do with it, Timmy. It was all in the planning, their meticulous attention to detail. Those blokes are geniuses. They had every right to be confident they'd never get caught. You've got to respect blokes who can pull off a brazen daylight robbery.

Through Ross, I began to grasp a key tenet of police psychology; The Myth of The Criminal Mastermind. The Criminal Mastermind is to frustrated police what alien abduction is to the spiritually confused.

According to this myth, the imbeciles, deadheads, and psychotics who uniformly grace police records are balanced by an undetectable circle of Criminal Masterminds, criminals the police are powerless to apprehend.

The Criminal Mastermind is the criminal who cannot be caught, *by definition*. Nothing could convince police who subscribe to this myth that a deadhead could get lucky, that an imbecile could evade detection, that a psychotic would not ultimately give himself away. Nothing could persuade such a police officer that the bizarre concept of Criminal Masterminds is a rationalisation of the inadequacies of law enforcement, that it's a mythology of convenience.

9. God

Because all history is ultimately the history of provisional knowledge, ignorance, and irony, we shouldn't be too harsh on the Senior Constable who wrote of one sixteen-year-old offender:

> This boy operates under a mistaken belief that he is
> something special because two of his brothers play League

football, but you can rest assured that he'll never amount to anything more than a legend in his own mind.

After some consideration, I decided to save this prediction for posterity. The brash young offender in question was already in the process of becoming the footballer who would be universally revered as 'God'.

10. Pushing Eternity Uphill

During the four-and-a-half months I spent as the Bat Phone operator, I obliterated several thousand dangerously contentious predictions, estimations, and opinions. Though I knew this would not be my life's mission, that I would be returning to full-time study the following year, I never really warmed to the task. I might have preferred to see the officer–authors forced to take responsibility for their frankly expressed judgments. And, at another level, I felt part of me being eroded. I needed to balance this constant erasure and eradication with a creative act.

When Ross was in the toilet, or off collecting money, I began to manufacture history.

I opened a new file, and fabricated a detailed criminal history for a nonexistent arch criminal named M. Meursault. In keeping with his atheistic, antisocial outlook, M. Meursault had no Christian name as such, but sometimes passed under the twin aliases of The Stranger, or Sisyphus.

Found guilty of Crimes against God, and an Aggravated Assault on Metaphysics, M. Meursault had been sentenced to 'push eternity uphill'. His was a file that I would slip quietly among the tens of thousands of authentic files. It was a file that would never be accessed, and any justice in M. Meursault's obscure punishment would never be seen to be done.

In the process of creating M. Meursault, I gradually began to see my editorial task in a new light. Just as Camus had said of Sisyphus that we need to imagine him happy, that we should imagine Sisyphus as a man who would find a way to relish his eternal punishment, I tried to imagine myself as someone who was engaged in constructing a more hopeful, optimistic world. My liquid paper didn't only come to the defence of those who ought to have known better, I saw it having a magical, liberating effect on the criminal recipients of my godlike largesse.

As thrice-convicted burglar X moves between the supermarket and his run-down station wagon, he feels unaccountably lighter. He smiles at a stranger, the first time that he has done so since he was a young boy. He smiles with no thought of return or profit. X will never understand that this aberrant behaviour coincides exactly with my obliteration of the statement 'will certainly continue to re-offend'. He is about to begin again, to become the author of his own history. If he needs a title for that volume, I would suggest that it be called *The Remote Possibility of Happiness*.

STILL LIFE WITH LAMINGTONS

From the café, I could see Jack standing with an old man at the end of the pier. They were pointing up at the ferry timetables. Arms were flying about all over the place, and you couldn't tell whether they were arguing or joking. Jack shook his head, then the old man shook his head. Finally, Jack put his hand on the old man's shoulder and headed up the pier. He called out to me as he neared the café.

You can see why this place is the home of philosophy. It's totally fucked.

Aren't there any ferries?

Oh yeah, there are ferries all right. But no direct ferries from here to Meskos. The old bloke reckons the only way you can get to Meskos is to take the Trykos ferry. Even that stops at seven or eight dipshit islands before it gets to Trykos. And the ferry from Trykos to Meskos only runs every third day . . . Where's the logic? Meskos is twenty times the size of the other islands—you can practically swim to it from here—but there's no fucking ferry.

Yeah, these people are very thingy about Meskos. After Perseus escaped the minotaur, he was going to meet up with his betrothed on Trykos, but the sirens tricked him into swimming to Meskos where Demosthenes had him emasculated and sold off as a slave to the Trojans. You couldn't get anyone here to take a direct ferry to Meskos.

Jack belted back the last of his red wine and looked me in the eye.

You just made that up.

Well, sure. What do you want me to say? Of course there's no fucking ferry to Meskos. This place is fourth world.

We were quiet for a while after that. My brother and I had been travelling for more than sixty hours. Neither of us had slept or shaved. It was impossible to understand why it might take another two days to get to an island just four kilometres off the coast.

We'll have to pay one of these fishermen.

Yeah. Fuck it.

I held up my empty glass to see whether Jack wanted another one.

Dick, you don't have to go through with this if you don't want to. Mum and Dad wouldn't hold it against you. You could tell them there wasn't a ferry, that the signs weren't auspicious.

Nah, we've come this far. And I'm curious.

Well, this isn't a book you can close when the story doesn't interest you any more. It might be your last chance to back out.

I could hear someone inside the café dropping coins into the jukebox and hitting buttons to make their selection. I might have expected to hear Nana Mouskouri, or some drug-soaked rimbetica, but the song was *Love Will Tear Us Apart* by Joy Division. Jack was right. The signs weren't auspicious.

* * *

There was a time when I was suspended in time like a mosquito in jelly. No perspective at all. I was so panicked about the future that the present ceased to exist. To save myself from suffocation, I shut off all emotional engagement with the world.

Is it really possible to love someone too much, or is that just a romantic excuse invented by the lover who failed to love well enough?

I loved Miranda Murray so much I couldn't stand the thought that she might not always love me. The most minute conflict or misunderstanding became the portent of a disaster to come. So I shut off my emotions and sent her away, my panic disguised as cool decisiveness. When I finally realised what I had done, it was too late to remedy the situation.

Time, Mirandaless time, existed only to be obliterated.

I convinced myself that hard work was good for the soul, and I worked with a furious intensity. I knew that the intensity was more important than the work itself. I needed to be so far inside time that time would cease to have meaning, would cease to correspond with the world beyond my desk. I wrote, and wrote, and rewrote. And when I paused to look up from the page, two years had passed without me being aware they had passed. Worse, Miranda was still gone.

It was only when I reacquainted myself with banal, common-sense time that the crying started. I was thirty-seven years old.

It's excruciating to be bailed out of a psychiatric hospital by your elderly parents, to have your emotional life dragged into a public domain, to find yourself on the receiving end of so much warmth and sound advice.

What you should do is find yourself a nice girl and get married, my mother told me.

Thanks, Mum, you're absolutely right. Tomorrow . . . No. Tomorrow's Good Friday. I'll find myself a nice girl and get married straight after the holidays.

Just because everyone had been so patient with me didn't mean that I'd abandoned the right to be sarcastic. Other than doctors, nurses, and shop assistants, I hadn't spoken to a woman I didn't know for more than three years. The thought of lifelong partnership was just a little abstract. But Mum refused to be put off.

Look, Richard, you can choose not to be happy if you want to. No-one's saying that you have to find joy in things that don't make you joyful. But that's different from choosing unhappiness as a way of life. Some people choose to be unhappy because they're frightened they'll feel lost when they're happy.

You've sold me, Mum. I'm getting married. Go out and buy yourself an expensive dress.

I'm serious, Richard. You have a lot of love to give someone.

I'm overflowing with love and eligibility, but I don't see women beating a path to the front door.

You should meet Elizabeth Colley. Elizabeth Colley is a very beautiful girl.

Who is Elizabeth Colley?

Max and Gwen's daughter.

Mum, Max and Gwen live in Greece.

I'll show you her photograph. Gwen sent me a photo with her letter last Christmas.

Mum rummaged through a drawer in the kitchen and returned with a photograph of the thirty-two-year-old Elizabeth Colley. A man's idea of a beautiful woman seldom coincides with his mother's idea of a beautiful woman, but I had to admit that Elizabeth Colley answered my mother's description: serene and lovely, with a soft, shy smile, and glorious long red hair.

Yeah, nice try Mum, but you can't tell me that someone who looks like that has spent all her life waiting to meet a dickhead like me.

* * *

There is one thing I should make clear at this point. I never considered that what I was doing was involving myself in an arranged marriage. I never thought of it like that. I would have recoiled at the suggestion.

* * *

If you ever visit Meskos, don't forget your sunglasses. Blinding light bounces off white stone buildings packed onto the steep hills which rise above the port. According to my guidebook, Meskos is the largest and most populous island in its group, but it's hard to say what people do to earn a living. The fishermen spend more time in cafés than they do in their boats, and the locals have made no effort to develop the island as a tourist destination. Many less attractive islands do substantially more tourist business.

My father said that Western intelligence agencies use the island for satellite tracking and information gathering. While there's no shortage of high antennas and dishes on Meskos, we never encountered other foreigners, let alone military personnel or obvious CIA types. And I don't recall seeing an area where entry was restricted. The islanders appear relaxed, prosperous, and happy. The presence of two Australians didn't seem to bother them.

Everyone knew the Colleys. Max and Gwen had lived there forty years. Max had been one of the two doctors on the island till he retired seven years earlier. Being six-foot-six and Australian would have been enough to make him stand out even without all his quirks.

Kind old people stopped to explain the route to the Colley house. They drew maps in the dirt. They told us that it was much too far to carry suitcases. Island people often have a distorted sense of scale. Gwen's letter said that they lived a mile and a half from the port, though the hills were certainly steep enough to keep you honest.

How will we know which house is his? Jack asked Dad.

141

Oh, I'm pretty sure you'll know where you are when you get to the Colleys' house.

Which was true, as it turned out, but we were almost led astray. Nearing a crossroad, we encountered two exquisite girls: dark hair, tight black fashion jeans, luminous blouses. They couldn't have been older than twenty, and neither would have looked out of place flitting between the boutiques in Chapel Street. They smiled at us, and their eyes sparkled with all the right sorts of incitation.

Will we see you at the disco tonight? the girl in the hot-pink blouse asked. Good music. Hash. Coke. Whatever you want.

I could see that Jack wanted to say yes. He had momentarily forgotten that he was a married man and, for the purposes of this venture, my chaperone. I spoke for him.

Sounds great. But it depends . . . Do you know Elizabeth Colley?

I could hear them both giggling as they walked away.

Holy shit! Jack said, looking back over his shoulder, determined not to miss a single wiggle. Whoo! We've come to the right place!

The Colley house could not have been other than the Colley house.

A fence of unpainted wooden railings enclosed a large bushy block. The garden was dense with eucalypts and flowering gums which nearly obscured a weatherboard house. Surrounding the house on all sides was a broad veranda. A slanting roof of red corrugated iron. Television aerial on one side, tall mast with an Australian flag fluttering on the other.

A powerfully attractive cooking smell wafted out of the house, and I could hear the moan of the north wind as it passed through the wires of a Hills Hoist in the backyard.

* * *

Dad met Max Colley in 1945. They were young doctors with the occupational forces in Japan. Even though the two men are the same age, it's probably fair to say Dad hero-worships Max. Max was a brilliant footballer and a potential Wimbledon champion. If you speak to people who knew Max the sportsman, they always tell you, Max Colley could have been anything.

My father's Japanese experiences saw him veer towards the peace movement and left-of-centre politics, but Max headed in the other direction. I've never understood how people can maintain friendships with ideological opponents, but Dad managed to stay in touch with Max as he went first to Washington then back to Korea. Dad rejects the idea that his best friend was working for the CIA. He insists that The Company would have had Max spend more time in Australia if he had been an operative.

As it happens, Max did spend long periods of time in Australia during the 1950s, just as the Cold War was shifting into top gear. We have scrapbook photos of Uncle Max hitting up with Lew Hoad and Ken Rosewall. Dad reckons that if Max had been CIA his mission would have been to nobble Hoad and Rosewall.

During one of those return visits, Dad introduced Max to one of Mum's schoolfriends, Gwen Lester, and the couple got married after a whirlwind romance. Gwen was a trained nurse. According to Dad, Max had the idea that he and Gwen would take medical expertise into the third world, but they only got as far as the Greek islands before falling in love with Meskos.

To my knowledge, Max and Gwen have left Meskos just once since 1958. They returned to Australia in the mid-sixties to finalise Elizabeth's adoption. When they found they were unable to have children, Mum used her connections to stitch up a deal. Even on that trip, Max and Gwen breezed in and out of Melbourne. They signed the papers, had their baby daughter christened in Scots church, and left on the next boat. Jack and I attended Elizabeth's christening, but neither of us remember anything about it. Which is a pity, because it was a social event. The new Prime Minister Harold Holt was there. Apparently, Holt offered Max Colley a major diplomatic posting, but Max declined. He said that his work in Meskos meant everything to him. If you speak to people who knew conservative politics in the fifties and sixties, they always tell you, Max Colley could have been anything.

* * *

Bugger me with a stick, wouldya look at these two! You, you're just the image of yer old man. Come in, come in. You blokes must be totally scroted. It's a bloody long haul from Melbourne to Meskos. Don't know where Gwen and Lizzie have got to. Just sit tight and I'll fetch you a beer.

My hand was still throbbing from Max's grip. He was the most energetic seventy-five-year-old that I've met. A bald, Herculean giant, part-Chips Rafferty, part-Monsieur Hulot, trying to leave the room in two different directions at once.

Jack was examining the damage to his own hand. Did Max really use the phrase 'totally scroted'? he asked.

We heard Max in a distant room calling out to his wife and daughter, but heard no response. Every time Max moved, he sent vibrations through the large house.

Gwen, Lizzie! Get out here, the place has been invaded by young bronzed gods.

I can't say that I'd ever been referred to as a young bronzed god. Jack has a definite bronze about him, but I'm more often likened to Transylvanian aristocracy.

Max's voice bellowed from the kitchen, Richmond Bitter all right for you blokes?

Jack and I raised eyebrows in perfect synchrony. My brother called back, Yeah, no worries.

144

Richmond Bitter?

I don't reckon they've brewed the stuff since 1962, Jack said. We might be in for a treat.

'We might be in for a treat' was a phrase Jack used whenever cruel and unusual punishment was in the offing.

More crashing from another room, Orr, bugger it!

I'd seen houses much like the Colleys' house before, back when my family used to visit elderly relatives living in northern Victoria. Polished floorboards, a massive living room lined with bookcases spilling over with old hardbacks. Big cabinets full of crystal and Wedgwood. Old reclining chairs covered in red vinyl. Framed black-and-white photos of old family members, and a large colour-tinted photograph of the Queen. The same photograph of the Queen used to hang on the wall at Hampton Primary. A big piano in one corner, a television covered over with a blue towel in the other.

Finally, traces of conversations from a distant room.

Where on earth have you been? The boys are here. I've been trying to rustle up something to eat.

When Max returned, he was balancing a tray laden with three massive cans of Richmond Bitter. The cans were made of steel. The quantity of beer they contained was measured in fluid ounces, and Max had used a can-opener to rip the tops off dog-food style.

I don't expect that you boys will be fussed about glasses. Gwen will be with us in a jiff. Young Lizzie's gone off to get herself tizzed-up.

We raised our cans to acknowledge Max. The cans were so heavy that both hands were needed to perform the task, and they were frighteningly cold. They might have spent thirty-five years huddled in a refrigerator, waiting for this moment of publication.

I save the Richmond for special occasions . . . Tell me if it isn't the best drop you've ever knocked back.

To me it tasted like beer that had spent thirty-five years

doing whatever beer does in a steel can. Jack's the beer connoisseur, but his pupils were spinning out of control. That might have been three days without sleep as much as the beer. And we'd shared a cone with the fisherman who'd brought us over to Meskos. Maybe the whole Meskos experience was hallucination: the local girls, Max's folk museum, everything.

Seeing that Jack had flaked, Max moved forward to address me earnestly.

Bet you can't wait to set eyes on our Lizzie. She's not a very worldly girl, but she's a treasure. We should have fixed her up with an Australian lad years ago, but her mum and I have never been able to stomach the thought of being without her. She's a bonzer lass. She's talked of nothing but you coming since we got your mum's letter.

Jack heard none of this. The beer had demolished him. Maturity must have increased the alcohol content of the Richmond Bitter. It was all I could do to hold my eyelids open.

Finally, Gwen appeared. Though seventy or thereabouts herself, Gwen was a tall, elegant woman, quite striking. She was carrying a tray of plates piled high with fresh scones and pikelets.

Gwen was a little flustered. She introduced herself to Jack, and failed to notice that he was comatose. She'd start a sentence but fail to finish it. Not for the first time, I was told I was the dead spit of my father.

You'll have to excuse Elizabeth. She'll be with us in a minute, Gwen said. You took us by surprise.

Though I was flagging badly, I did my best with the food mountain. Max quizzed me about the recent form of the Essendon football team, and the current state of Australian tennis, while Gwen wanted to know about my family. Jack contributed nothing more than the occasional splurt.

Make sure you eat those scones while they're hot. A scone that can't melt butter is poison.

I hadn't eaten a fresh scone since the invention of the microwave oven. They were sensational scones, but my head was swimming. While Max disappeared to fetch more beer, I tried to explain to Gwen that Jack and I were experiencing critical sleep deficit. In doing so, I knocked a saucer off the coffee table, and the clatter on the uncarpeted floorboards sent a cat scurrying out from under the couch, momentarily shaking Jack from his hibernation.

As I apologised, Max returned with the beer, and following close behind him, carrying a tray loaded with cupcakes and lamingtons, was his daughter.

Elizabeth Colley was even more lovely in the flesh than the photograph I had seen. She wore a white blouse, a tartan skirt of green and blue to just above the knee, and dark blue stockings. She was tall, with high cheeks, the prettiest mouth, long waves of magnificent red hair, and soft, pale skin which looked like it had never seen the sun.

When Max introduced Elizabeth, I shook her hand and said that it was a pleasure to meet her. Elizabeth said nothing in reply, but released a serene half-smile which sent a flush through her cheeks.

Make sure you try one of Lizzie's lamingtons. You won't find a better lamington on Meskos.

Since no one else was eating anything, I took it as my duty to eat three lamingtons while Max and Gwen nattered about the grand days of sea travel, and the silent Elizabeth measured my reactions. With each lamington, I tried to be more enthusiastic than I had been previously. And they were top-drawer lamingtons; freshly desiccated coconut, dark chocolate, and much fresher cake than a lamington-eater has the right to expect. But my pupils were doing three-sixties, and somewhere between the third lamington and the second cupcake, I joined my brother in unconsciousness.

* * *

During the days which followed, Jack made himself scarce by wandering off down to the port. He said that this was to give Elizabeth and I the chance to be alone together, though really he meant to avoid the stupendous quantities of food produced in the Colley kitchen.

The sight of Elizabeth made my heart quiver, but getting her to stay still or say something required more diplomatic skill than I possessed. No sooner would I contrive a situation where we shared the same space than Max wandered in to abduct me.

Even in retirement, Max lived a vigorously active life. He insisted that I play tennis with him. Tennis is not my game. I have no serve, and my backhand is so feeble I have to switch grips and play left-handed forehands. Max was still a formidable opponent, and his game was made all the more daunting by the peculiarities of his home court.

Max Colley's tennis court is one of the twentieth century's finest examples of arsehole architecture. Everything was designed to protect Max's invincibility.

I ought to have guessed something was up when my host unveiled a home rule which decreed that ends would not be changed. The end closest to the house belonged to Max, owing to his need to hear the phone. Naturally, his end was beautifully shaded, while I found myself looking directly into the sun. What's more, the red gravel surface, rolled smooth as a freeway on Max's side of the net, was strewn with large stones on mine. Not immediately apparent to the untrained or trusting eye was an M.C. Escher technique used to mark the lines. Perspective had been artfully distorted so that Max's opponents defended an area fifty per cent larger than his. While Max rarely needed to move for anything, I would have had to sprint for ten seconds to cover the baseline. Cruellest of all was a wicked camber which always directed the ball away from my lunging racquet. Max's guests were asked to defend a very large, lumpy car bonnet.

I might be a lousy player, but I'm proud and competitive. I certainly didn't intend to be humiliated by a man I wanted to impress. Max couldn't have cared less about my humiliation. He talked the whole match through, knowing I was too breathless to respond.

You'll have to work on that backhand, Richard. I used to hit up with Kenny Rosewall. Kenny had a bugger of a good backhand.

A top-spun lob came straight out of the sun and hit me above the right ear.

I might have given Kenny and Lew a run for their money in their prime. But those lads had the good fortune to have their prime after the War.

A wicked smash hit one of the larger stones and kicked away at a right angle. Max showed no obvious sign of embarrassment or sympathy.

If you ask me, Australians have an unfair advantage. It might even be genetic. Look at Ron Clarke, and Murray Rose, and Dawn Fraser.

A drop volley looped over the net. The net seemed to be fifty metres away, and my legs were jelly. I was too gutted to wave a handkerchief in surrender.

More likely it's the outdoor life. Australian youngsters don't wait for someone to entertain them. They're always swimming, or running, or kicking a ball. You never see that with these lads here on Meskos. If it's not the plonk, it's drugs, or loud music. And most of the girls are just made-up trollops . . . Excuse the French, but what else can you say? . . . They're out to all hours of the night, and their parents don't seem to care. If unmarried girls had abortions in Australia like they do here on Meskos, there'd be a scandal. Church leaders would stamp down on it, or there'd be a Royal Commission. But it could never get like that in Australia, because Australian parents care about their children. They teach them self-discipline, and family values.

Here, all the kids get taught is how to expect something for nothing.

A perfectly dinked backhand landed on the line and scooted away down the hill. Before I could get to the net to shake hands, Max called out, What say we make it best of five?

I'm not going to lie to you, Richard. Gwen and I will miss Lizzie terribly. But you two will be wanting to have children, and Australia's the only place for that . . . Things have changed on Meskos. There used to be a local culture. Now, it might as well be America. People only seem to care about gambling, and getting smashed. We've done our best to make sure Lizzie's never been contaminated by any of that. I like to think that we've brought her up to be a fine young lady.

A forehand volley at the net hit me square in the testicles. It was all that I could do not to vomit.

Hey, take care of those! You might have my grandsons swimming about in there!

I had the feeling that Max's grandsons and I were caught in a very strong current.

* * *

Dinner had to be postponed half an hour owing to Jack's late return from the village. I recognised instantly that he was stoned, and hoped the fact would elude our hosts. Just the task of tucking in his serviette brought on an uncontrollable burst of giggling.

This is one of Elizabeth's specialities, Gwen announced. I hope you boys like mock chicken casserole.

Mock chicken, Jack said. *Mock* chicken.

Another burst of giggling. I kicked Jack's leg under the table, trying to calm him down.

Mmm, it's delicious, I said.

Strong flavour. You must grain-feed the chooks here, Jack added.

Your dad and I used to go out shooting in the Mallee, Max said.

Before he got any further, Jack hammered the handle of his fork into the table, in a poor attempt to feign indignation. Max, I hope you're not intending to impugn my father as a *mock* chicken hunter . . .

Jack . . .

Did he mock, or did he hunt?

It's an old-fashioned way of saying rabbit, Jack, I explained.

Jack stopped as if shot. Generally he made a point of not eating cuddly things.

You're a fabulous cook, Elizabeth, I said, trying to draw her into the conversation.

Lizzie knows Mrs Beeton backwards, Gwen answered.

I'm sure we'd all like to know Mrs Beeton backwards, Jack said, this time to the obvious annoyance of Max, who knew crude double entendre when he heard it.

You seem to be having a lot of fun down in the village, Jack.

They have a pretty wild social scene in town, Jack said. Do you get down there much, Liz?

No she doesn't, her father answered. The young blokes down there might seem like fun, but they're hopeless bludgers. Pack of bodgies the lot of them.

Bodgies, Jack repeated.

Elizabeth was removing our plates.

What's for pud, Lizzie? Max asked.

Lizzie's made a beautiful jam rolypoly, Gwen said.

Oh, that sounds fantastic, I said, but I couldn't eat another thing.

Lizzie's gone to a lot of trouble, Max said. Never discourage a girl who takes trouble with her rolypoly.

* * *

151

I had the top bunk, and Jack had the bottom bunk. Even in our thirties, he pulled rank.

Jack, you can't come back here stoned.

Can't you speed things up with Lizzie? We've got to get out of here. These people don't know the meaning of cholesterol. I'm starting to shit whipped cream.

If she's not cooking with Gwen in the kitchen, Max is dragging me off to discuss Arthur Calwell and Frank Sedgman. Max thinks the whole thing is a *fait accompli*.

If everything's decided, get her back to Melbourne, and start making babies.

Jack, I haven't even heard her speak except to say, Would you like more cream with that?

Hey, when a woman looks like her, that's all she needs to say.

Lizzie's dead stunning all right, but I can't see her rollicking in the bedroom. She'll belong to the lie back and think of Canberra school.

Bullshit! These reserved, conservative girls are always the ones that turn out best value once they're wound up.

I dunno.

Dick, you've got to find out pronto. We can't stay here forever. Not with the mock scones and mock goats. You two are making a fucking mockery of courtship.

* * *

When I finally did hear Elizabeth's voice, it was her singing voice.

After Sunday roast, Max insisted that we sing around the piano. Lizzie sang with a sweet purity that was touching. She seemed to know all the old Irish and Australian folksongs, but nothing written since Richie Benaud was a boy.

Why don't you sing us something, Richard?

I can't sing, and I can't play.

Since when does that matter?

As it happens, I love singing, but I have no singing voice. So I sang a very nervous, flat rendition of a Matt Johnson song. The subconscious mind is a tricky bastard. I'd chosen the first song that came to mind, and only when I began to sing the chorus did I realise its strange appropriateness. It came over as a declaration of intent. My life needed to change, and this was the day when it was going to change.

I saw Elizabeth watching me, running her teeth over her lower lip. I wanted to grab her and kiss her.

That was lovely, Gwen said. Richard deserves a treat.

Elizabeth scurried off to the kitchen to retrieve a massive pavlova, the whipped cream packed with banana and passionfruit. While Elizabeth was gone, Max tidied away her sheet music. He was desperately sad.

She's a bonzer girl that one. You'll take good care of her, won't you Richard?

I'm sure he will, Gwen added.

* * *

Elizabeth's pavlova was an item of such delicacy and brilliance that I might have proposed marriage on the spot. A woman with that kind of control over a large meringue crust is capable of anything.

Eventually, Gwen went off to take a nap, and Max dragged a very reluctant Jack out onto the tennis court, leaving Elizabeth and I alone in the sitting room. While I examined the bookshelves, she worked on a patchwork quilt.

Do you have a favourite writer, Elizabeth?

Jane Austen and Tolstoy are my all-time favourites, but mostly I read Australian authors.

Yeah? Who do you like?

Henry Lawson, Barbara Baynton, Eleanor Dark, Kenneth Slessor.

How about *modern* Australian writers?

I like some of George Johnston . . . *My Brother Jack* is good.

You should read Beverley Farmer. She's written beautiful stories about a young Australian woman living in Greece.

Greece has never really interested me. It's only Australia that I know about.

Things have changed a bit since Max and Gwen last saw Australia.

Not nearly as much as they've changed here. Things change so much it makes you dizzy. You wonder if people actually believe in anything, if there's anything worth holding onto. Australians would never be so negative about the future. They're much more hopeful. No-one on Meskos ever hopes for anything more than money.

* * *

So did you and young Lizzie have a good chat about things?

Max stripped the top off another steel can while Jack went upstairs to die.

I should show you around the studio.

When Max retired from daily medical practice, he took up painting. He warned me beforehand that he was a beginner, telling me I shouldn't be too harsh in my judgment. He was still trying to clarify his artistic vision.

To be honest, I was shocked. I had expected fey tradition-alism, or landscapes, but Max had a vigorous expressionistic technique, not quite so pared back as de Kooning, but broad, powerful brushstrokes and abrasive colours.

These are really wild, Max.

Wild, yes, that's probably the right word for them. I'd like them to be wilder, angrier.

I'm no critic, but I could see that Max was a better artist than he gave himself credit for. He described most of his works as preliminary studies, but they looked like finished paintings to me.

This is my favourite, he said. 'Evil begets evil.'

Two naked males appeared to be locked in a fight to the death.

It's a tag-team wrestling match. That's Doc Evatt, and that's B.A. Santamaria. Santamaria's trying to tag Frank McManus in the blue corner, but Doc is pulling him back . . . Hard times, Dick. If the Commos or the Micks had got their way, Australia would have been buggered. Thank Christ we had big Bob holding the show together with some common bloody sense. Australians probably wish Menzies was still running the show.

Some do . . . Do you keep track of what's going on in Australia, Max?

You don't get a lot of Australian news here on Meskos . . . Never enough to get the full picture. To me, the worst thing was when they went and changed the currency. How could the Liberals countenance a treachery like that? It was one thing to go decimal, but there was no need to change the names. What was wrong with pounds, shillings and pence? . . . Don't get me wrong. I love the Yanks. They won the War for us, but we don't have to live like them. We're bloody lucky our Lizzie's a pounds and shillings girl.

How do you mean?

Elizabeth was born on February 13th, 1966. Made it by a day . . . It would have been nice if she'd been born while R.G. was running the show, but Menzies was still top man when she was conceived, and that's the main thing.

I could offer no sensible response to this. I suddenly had the terrible idea that Elizabeth might be Menzies' love child, that Menzies was quite literally the top man when she was conceived.

Stick with me for a tick, I've got a portrait of R.G. and Dame Patty here somewhere.

Max flicked his way through a pile of canvases stacked up against the wall. I was worried that Menzies and Dame Patty might be depicted in a nude tag-team wrestling match.

You know, I'm not sure that I could go back now. Dollars. Taxes on petrol. Professional tennis . . . Still, I've heard that this young bloke Howard is top-shelf. He's not the kind of man who'd let the bodgies intimidate him.

* * *

I had peculiar dreams. I made brief trips back home to Hampton to check my answering machine and collect the mail. The only items waiting for me were carefully boxed cakes posted by Elizabeth. They were magnificent productions: Strawberry Cream Torte, and Raspberry Temptation. The cakes ought to have been photographed, they demanded immortalisation, but they were inedible. The whipped cream hadn't travelled well.

* * *

Three weeks passed. Jack and I lost the need to use belts. Life with the Colleys was like the revenge of Margaret Fulton. Nothing slowed the lamington production line: honey-coated lamingtons, cherry ripe lamingtons, rocky road lamingtons.

Between the lamingtons, there were tarts and dumplings, pies and pastries. Yorkshire puddings. Casseroles by the troughful. While Jack and I began to look like badly constipated Sumo wrestlers, the Colleys remained slender and elegant. Either they had high-speed metabolic processing, or they were secretly bulimic.

Jack and I were never permitted to carry a dish or enter the kitchen. This secrecy about the kitchen led us to imagine a room like Dr Who's Tardis, a room that cheated space and time. Where did the fresh bananas and strawberries come from? Where was the silo which held the Colleys' stockpile of desiccated coconut? You wouldn't have dared open the deepfreeze for fear that you'd find Heather McKay or Norm O'Neill being cryogenically preserved.

Jack let out a tremendous fart which sent a shudder through the bunkbeds.

Lad, you've got to bring matters to a head with Liz. We're cooking up a dental emergency. I want to see my kids again before I die.

* * *

I tried to imagine what Elizabeth might be thinking, what she could be hoping for, and whether I might correspond to the kind of man she hoped for. I tried to imagine what it might be like to live with Elizabeth in Melbourne, and how such a sheltered woman would react to a city so different to anything within her experience. Though she had been taught at home, Liz was bright and capable. But the thing was, she'd been brought up to become someone's wife, and wives are no longer the kind of wives that Elizabeth had been trained to become.

Could such a woman be deprogrammed, or *want* to be deprogrammed? Did she dream of making scones for rugged firefighters, or surf lifesavers? Maybe she dreamt of moving among a crowd of sophisticated people who sipped sherry and discussed Eleanor Dark and A.D. Hope. How would I know if she'd have the patience or desire to deal with someone who had been so fucked in the head as I had been?

Elizabeth Colley was highly desirable, much more attractive than she knew. She was also inscrutable.

* * *

Do you swim, Richard?

I had been reading *The Tree of Man*. Elizabeth was sewing. Never before had she initiated conversation.

I love the water, but I'm not a strong swimmer.

Are there beaches near where you live?

There are terrific beaches at Sandringham and Black Rock, and there are fabulous ocean beaches an hour's drive away.

I might have mentioned sharks, the coldness of the water, ozone depletion, and skin cancer, all my usual fears, but we were on a roll.

You can't swim on the beaches here. The islanders get drunk and swim naked.

I could picture Elizabeth swimming naked, her red hair sweeping down toward a magnificent bare arse, her long legs spreading and closing. The erotic charge of it left me giddy enough to joke.

I'm too shy to swim naked. I like to keep my tatts where people can't see them.

Tattoos? Elizabeth was scandalised. Only sailors and criminals have tattoos. You don't really have tattoos, do you?

No. I hate tatts. They're gauche . . . But I do have a silver stud through my clitoris.

I waited for a smile, or a scowl, but there was neither.

What's a clitoris?

* * *

My parents never really liked the girls I brought home, but they did their best. They wanted to see me with a girl who would devote herself to supporting me, but I was always attracted to brilliant, independent women like Miranda Murray, women with loads of ambition and character, girls who were practically certain to discard me in the course of time.

Even though I brought it on myself, Mum and Dad hated

158

to see me hurt. I'm sure they would have been thrilled if I'd come home with a pretty, old-fashioned girl like Elizabeth Colley, a young woman who had been educated to value pleasantness above all else.

But my parents have absorbed enough modern influences to agree with me on one matter—I'm talking about implicit agreement here, it's definitely not the kind of thing we discuss. They would accept that an intelligent, thirty-two-year-old woman on the verge of entering married life should have a better than fair idea what a clitoris is.

If I wanted to back out, I now had an excuse. But I didn't know what I wanted. Neither did I know what Elizabeth wanted. I thought I knew what Elizabeth expected me to want.

I've spent most of my adult life cultivating a low level of expectation, a level of underachievement I could easily live down to. The people who knew me expected little from me, and I generally chose to do no more than they expected me to do.

* * *

Gwen Colley had very little to say on most issues. Cooking, sweeping, sewing, and stretching canvases for Max seemed to be her life. I found it hard to imagine her as the same woman who had kept up regular correspondence with my mother for forty years. But finally it was Gwen who put foot to the pedal.

I think Lizzie's expecting you to speak to her, Richard. You mustn't expect Elizabeth to lead the way with these things. She's not as shy as you might think, but she does have a strict sense of propriety and etiquette.

I understood all this to mean that Elizabeth was waiting for me to propose a future life in Australia which involved marrying me, and that such an arrangement would have Max and Gwen's blessing.

I went to the bathroom to brush my teeth, bumping into my bloated brother as I left.

Dick, see if you can't have her packed and ready to leave by the end of the week.

I found Elizabeth sitting at the piano playing Beethoven. When she saw me enter, she smiled sweetly, and stopped playing.

You didn't have to stop.

Oh, I already know the rest.

Look, Liz, let's not beat around the bush. You must find this as awkward as I do. When Mum showed me your photograph, I was pretty certain you were my sort of girl. Then your folks made it clear that you would be interested to meet me. Well . . . I like you a lot, Liz. You're a very beautiful woman. A bloke'd be crazy or gay not to be attracted to you. I'm not going to pretend that this is what romance is all about. I'm never going to be wealthy or famous. I'm as ordinary as they come. But I'm honest. You're a sensible girl from a very fine family. If you'd like to, I think we could make a go of it.

Oh, Richard.

Believing this to be a so-grateful, prelude-to-tears 'Oh, Richard', I went on, as much to spare Lizzie's embarrassment as anything.

I'm sure that the financial side of things will work out. I could go back to writing for television till we're on track. Though you don't have any qualifications or experience, you're very intelligent and personable, and your dad has great connections. We could fudge a Greek *c.v.* and no-one would be the wiser.

Oh, Richard. I'm so sorry.

Sorry? . . . You don't want to come back to Australia with me?

You're a very nice fellow, but . . .

Look, you don't have to be in love with me, Liz. I used to be a romantic, but I don't trust that stuff now. Love is a muscle. If there's respect, and trust, and good will . . . I mean, these kind of arrangements often work famously, because people are determined to make them work.

It's just . . . You're not the kind of man I expected you to be.

Oh . . . What kind of man were you hoping for?

I expected you to be more . . . I don't know. More vigorous. More determined. More certain of yourself. Fearless and optimistic. You're very pleasant looking. You're kind. You're obviously quite clever. But you're open to some strange ideas. You're quite, susceptible, I think . . . I suppose that I expected you to be more Australian.

* * *

Susceptible? Yes, it was a fair cop. Susceptible to vibrant ideas. Novelty. Pretty women, always. To stillness, but a stillness that precedes motion. I am much too susceptible.

* * *

There's no direct ferry from Meskos to the Greek mainland. That hardly seemed to matter on the return journey.

Jack tried to comfort me, but I didn't really need comforting, so he found comfort in the company of a pretty Viennese art student who offered him some Turkish hash. She told Jack that the CIA used Meskos as a drug clearing-house for southern Europe.

They stood at the rear of the ferry, giggling and exchanging conspiracy theories, while Meskos slowly disappeared into the late-afternoon haze. I held my arms open to a faint cooling breeze, much like a primary school kid pretending to be a

161

tree swaying in the wind, and almost as happy. I was going somewhere.

When I got back to Australia, I was going to do all the things I'd never seriously thought about doing. Heroin. Group sex. I might even give golf a try. I was middle-aged and single. Maybe I'd always be single. But I was young enough— vibrantly young—and growing younger by the minute.

ACKNOWLEDGMENTS

I am most indebted to the Australian taxpayer for providing support through a Developing Writers grant from the Literary Board of the Australia Council.

'An Evening with Boo Radley' uses excerpts from the film *To Kill a Mockingbird* (1962)—Alan J. Pakula producer, with a script by Horton Foote from the novel by Harper Lee, and directed by Robert Mulligan for Brentwood Films. The article 'Quantum Physics and Motherhood' by Danah Zohar appears in *About Time*, edited by Christopher Rawlence (Jonathan Cape, London, 1985).

'Packing Death' and 'Duckness' first appeared in *Meanjin*. 'Steve Waugh . . . ' first appeared in *Certifiable Truths*, edited by Jane Messer (Allen & Unwin, 1998).

This collection probably wouldn't have existed in the absence of inspiration drawn from the works of Chris Marker, Andrey Tarkovsky, Jorge Luis Borges and Oliver Sacks.

I wish to thank those who read and commented on the work in manuscript: Louise Fox, Robert Adams, Ariane Rummery, Gus Braidotti, Judy Bourke, Peter Morrissey, Meaghan Delahunt and the friends and mentors who have supported me through this project.

Many thanks to Sophie Cunningham, Emily O'Connell, April Murdoch, Beth McKinlay, Carol Grabham and Annette Barlow, along with all those at Allen & Unwin.

Above all, I'd like to thank my family: Marjory and Alistair Richards, Margaret, David, Fiona and Kiera Berry, Jenny, Alistair, Campbell and Dylan Richards.